East End West End Kids

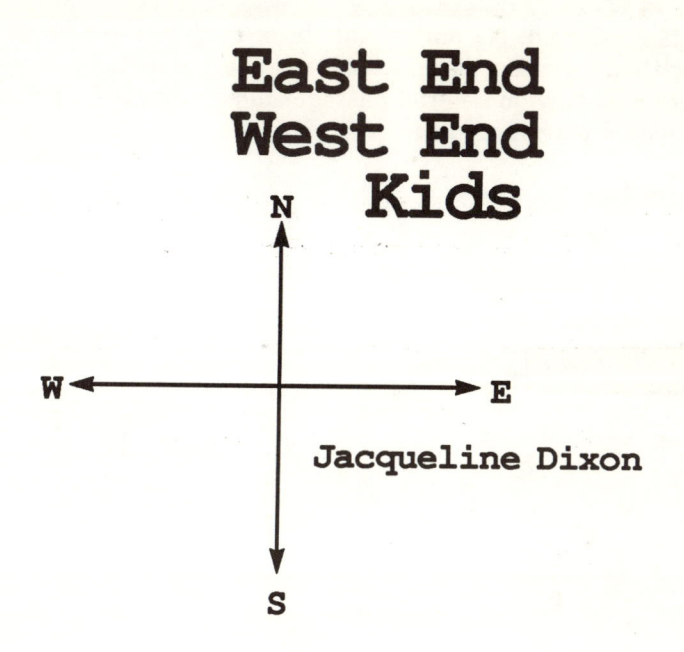

Jacqueline Dixon

Winston-Derek Publishers, Inc.
Pennywell Drive—P.O. Box 90883
Nashville, TN 37209

Copyright 1991 by Winston-Derek Publishers, Inc.

All rights reserved. No part of this book may be reproduced in any form without written permission from the publishers, except by a reviewer who may quote brief passages in a review to be printed in a newspaper or magazine.

First printing

PUBLISHED BY WINSTON-DEREK PUBLISHERS, INC.
Nashville, Tennessee 37205

Library of Congress Catalog Card No: 89-51345
ISBN: 1-55523-267-1

Printed in the United States of America

Acknowledgments

Kathaleen Williams, always like a mother to me, thanks for all of your advice and guidance. Don Bodey, my instructor at Columbia College in '82, thanks for giving me the confidence. Claire, your support meant the world to me and your friendship I will cherish forever. Thanks for your patience and understanding, especially to my closests, Eric D. Courtney and Kimberly Boyd. A special thank-you to Rev. Jessie Jackson for taking time out during the hectic mayoral election day to come by and pray with Mama; this was definitely a highlight in her life. And to all those at US AIR airlines who made it possible for Kelvin and his family to sporadically return home during Mom's illness—all of your kindness combined to give me a burst of energy, enabling me to continue with this book.

> I know you are hurting when you smile
> The things you do to me
> To me
> To me
> Makes me hurt when I smile
> Both hurting when we smile
> Makes a boring face.
>
> Jacqueline Dixon

To Mom, Dad, and all my brothers and sisters: Valerie, Toney, Jeanette, Kelvin, Reginald, Chris, John, and Juanita for being my best friends and simply yourselves.

In Memory of

Dear Mama,

    A few weeks after your surgery when I came over to take you out to dinner, you said that you didn't want to go because you weren't well enough. Remember how I kept telling you that it was all in your mind, that you would be all right, that the surgery had removed all the bad stuff from inside you? I kept trying to convince you to come outside and get some fresh air. You didn't budge. You knew that something was wrong. It was all over your face, all in your eyes. I was confident that your problem had become emotional and not physical, for only a couple of days ago all of your tests had come back negative, and your surgery was labeled a miraculous success.

    One night, after your readmittance, we had just come from being with you at the hospital. We were talking over dinner and Kelvin was telling Juanita and me that he really believed that you were going to leave us. He said that all his life, through all hardships you've faced, he had never once heard you say that you had had enough. Then as we had stood over your bed and were telling you to fight, you were telling us that you had had enough. You told us that you would try but that you couldn't make any promises. And after your occasional respiratory attacks you would often say, "If only I could just be quiet, if I could just be still." Juanita and I reflected back and realized that Kelvin had made a good point. However, I allowed everything that he had said to pass right through me. I didn't focus on the vision; I looked past the signs. I wasn't going to dare to accept that the grasp I had had on you all my life must give way.

As a child I often tried to take advantage of your passivity and was tickled pink by your innocence. I remember the few times you'd manage to build up enough courage to blurt out a curse word. We would all giggle and giggle. Your swear words were always under-pronounced and terribly accented. Profanity was not comfortable in your heart or mind. Your words were scarce, soft-spoken and hardly ever had exclamations behind them. All of my tree branch whippings came from Daddy. As an adult I came to appreciate your unconditional love and vast understanding of my imperfections. I came to admire the way you always gave and gave and gave but asked for so little in return.

You, lying there with your arm swollen up four times its normal size, your lungs clouding in on you. There you were facing such adversity and there you were—a person who didn't even know how to swear. I was so afraid for you, Mama. No matter how much we all stayed by your side, encouraged you to fight and gave you hope, *you* were the one lying inside that wasting body. I was so afraid for you, Mama. No matter how many times I kept telling you that your lungs were going to clear, you kept saying that you didn't think you were going to make it. I didn't listen to you; I didn't listen to anything. I had made a promise to myself at the onset of this thing that you were not going to die, that I would keep my faith till the end, that you would be healed. Mama, I was so afraid for you.

You seemed to be a little more comfortable being around us that Sunday although you hadn't even been home for a full week yet. You were so reluctant about coming home, feeling ashamed and like a burden because of the care you needed. As we took turns alongside your bed, Daddy fixed pancakes for breakfast. Sitting down in front of my stack, I thought how odd it was that Daddy had decided to fix pancakes on this morning. Jesus Christ, I thought, I couldn't remember the last time I had pancakes. When we were all living underneath the same roof, pancake breakfasts in our household meant family, togetherness, and lots of stuffed bellies. Funny thing, I didn't lose my appetite or grow cold at the thought. I ate my pancakes and got a stuffed belly. All of us who could be there on this Sunday morning sat down and got stuffed bellies. You were still being stubborn as you had been for the last couple of days: not eating your food, procrastinating to take your medication.

Reggie and I stood by your bedside and you began to speak. Your words weren't directed at us, but out into the open air. "I know what I want but. I know what I want, but." Your hand reached out. "But I don't have it yet." You opened your hand as if you were waiting for someone to place something in your palm. "But where is it? I don't have it yet. I know, I don't have . . . where is it? Pull that down. Pull where what I want." I panicked. I just knew now that it had spread to your brain, that you no longer had a grip on reality. Seeing your body disabled was one thing but seeing you leave us mentally was more than I felt that I could handle. I moved my fingers through your sweaty, soft and curly hair. Making certain not to bring my finger's quest to your attention, I came across that large lump that was beginning to get even larger. Someone had told me about it before but I tried to ignore this newfound bit of information and make it unimportant. But now it seemed to have hold on my undivided attention. There was never a mention about this thing on your part or ours but I am sure that you knew it was there. You kept looking at your bare wrist and asking what time it was, as if you had a scheduled appointment to make, and certainly you did. Again I didn't focus on the vision, I looked past the signs. As I watched you continuously seem disoriented, my hand shied away to the other side of your head where your scalp was smooth.

Standing there I began to feel like a lifeless, empty shell. My insides had no vitality to them. My heart wasn't beating anymore, I didn't even know if I was breathing or not. I could not feel my toes. I don't know how I was able to take this challenge but I looked down at you. "Mama, Mama who am I? Who am I?" I waited for my off-the-wall, oddball answer. You looked up at me, your thick eyebrows arched up high, "Jackie, Jackie! You're Jackie." I could feel myself inhaling and exhaling again. I was so elated, so alive again. For a moment I thought that your hallucinations might have been hallucinations only from my perspective. For a moment, I hoped that you would be given, from anyone speaking with you, whatever your hand sought so earnestly.

We told you that Father Pollard was coming and we granted your request to be moved from your bed to your recliner. He was due at 11:00 a.m. and it was fast approaching. Daddy didn't call Father over to give you your last rites because we actually believed that you needed them. Not soon, not today, not now anyway. We were all just getting ourselves organized, making out schedules to rotate during the coming weeks to make sure you would get the care that you needed. Giving you your last rites was just something we wanted to get out of the way. One of those just in case, but not really necessary at the moment, types of things. Yeah, so what, the doctors all said there was nothing more they could do for you, that you were at your end. We heard them. We sort of listened, relying on our faith that God was the real decision-maker. Anyway you had always been there for us—there to prepare our daily meals. Making your household your work-place, you didn't search the world for vain identities; rather you simply chose to be a mother—a hundred percent divine mother. Death could not have you—death would not have you—for we honestly could not recall a moment when you had denied us of your presence.

Father Pollard told you that all your sins had been forgiven, that if God called, you were indeed ready for your journey. You received the Eucharist and whispered amen. Immediately you adjusted yourself into your recliner, oh-so-proud-like. Whatever it was that you had needed, you seemed to have it now. As you lay back in your recliner fast asleep and with your arm all propped, I played around with the remote control to the television. I happened to catch the broadcast of an interview with Mother Theresa. The discussion was centered around poor people. She was saying how important it was to administer to the poor, yet at the same time to leave them with their self-respect and dignity, how important it was not to make them feel ashamed about being poor, needing, wanting. I questioned if there was any significance as to why I had happened to stumble onto this channel. Mother Theresa was talking about poor people. We had done everything we could to let you know that you weren't a burden to us. I didn't know. I simply couldn't make any relation to your predicament and to what this interview was all about. Something inside told me that there was some relation but I couldn't put my finger on it. I looked over at your hard, massive arm. Fluid was seeping onto the pillows from out of your pores. I suddenly lost interest in the conversation on television and concentrated on your suffering.

It was four in the evening. Your refusal to eat was really beginning to worry us. You couldn't fight if you didn't eat. Reggie put a spoonful of yogurt up to your mouth and without any hesitation you opened wide. Again you took another spoonful and another. I was so excited. Reggie wore a face of conquering. I hurriedly warmed some chicken and rice soup. Without any hesitation you opened wide. Reggie gave you your last pill. We were all so satisfied. You were fighting again, trying to stay alive, trying to stay with us.

Thirty minutes later I walked back into your room and heard Chris whisper that she thought you had stopped breathing for a moment. Wait a minute. What did you say? The day had not ended yet. I could still taste the pancakes on my breath from this morning's breakfast. I ran to get you a cold towel. I told Juanita in a low voice. Daddy was in the kitchen preparing dinner. I didn't want him to hear; I didn't want to startle him. Not more than two seconds had passed when I looked over my shoulder and saw Daddy standing there looking down at you. He knew right away. "She's leaving us, ya'll, she's leaving us. Oh Jesus!" I wanted to scream, to yell, to hold you, to try to motivate some life back into your failing body. Then that interview that I had seen earlier flashed into my mind.

Your spirit needed to be enriched and this was something that your poor body couldn't do. I swallowed my cries and I remained dry-eyed. As one needs self-respect and dignity to live, one also needs it to die. No one panicked, no one ran to call the ambulance, no one hollered. We remembered that you had said that you did not want to be resuscitated. Silenced, paralyzed in our shoes, we watched your big beautiful eyes dangle while you slowly drifted from behind them. There seemed to be nothing moving in that room except for you. Finally, at that moment we had let go totally of our selfishness to deny you of the glory that you so much deserved.

Your breaths were slow and quite intermittent. The next one seemed like it would never come, and finally it didn't. I was reminded of the way oxygen tanks sometimes sat useless while air was continuously pumped into one who didn't give it back. Your limp head rested back and your mouth opened a bit. I don't know why, but strangely I looked inside, where I saw the rice, the chicken bits, and the pill that Reggie had given to you, all nicely matted onto your palate. Oh, Mama, that was the greatest gift that you could have ever given to us. It will last us our lifetime. Thank you so much for appreciating all that we were trying to do for you. Thanks for coming home and letting us try to take care of you.

You didn't gasp for air; you didn't complain that you couldn't breathe as you had done so many times before. There were no tears streaming from your eyes; you made no uneasy movements. It just looked as though you were going off into a comfortable sleep.

So your spirit became enriched and vital. Your poor body remained with us and we prepared it without any disgrace. Intact remained your self-respect, intact remained your dignity. I am so proud that you didn't give in this time to our selfish wants, that you finally thought about yourself.

We have not lost our faith that you could have been healed physically. We only wrongly thought too hard that God would heal you in the way that we wanted. We, too, forgot who the real decision-maker was and had already chosen your destiny ourselves. God did more than heal you. God took you home. And in one's final moment there is truly no place, no place like home. You've always sat patiently and solid upon the Lord's rock. You knew you had earned your wings. I realize now that I was always so afraid—not for you Mama, but for myself.

1930-1989

Chapter 1

"Yo' kids ain't gon know shit about da funk monster."

"Listen, we decent folks around here. Could you please take yo' garbage talk elsewhere? We don't need that kinda talk around here." Daddy walked his slim and tall figure back over to the kitchen sink.

"Jus don't wonna face da facts, do ya?"

"The fact is you drunk!" Daddy exclaimed. "You full of that stuff. You don't know what end is at the top or which end is at the bottom. I know you, done went and filled yo'self up with dat stuff and den gon come try and tell me how da run my house."

Daddy was correct. Aunt Ruthie, Daddy's brother's girlfriend, was full of booze. Aunt Ruthie was a thin and tall woman in her early thirties. Her frequent visits to the liquor store earned her face an additional ten years. She, along with her two hundred forty pound friend, Wilma Troop, was supposed to be paying Mama a visit. As usual, Aunt Ruthie felt it was her duty to give Daddy a reading on his life. I liked Aunt Ruthie because she said things to Daddy that no one else dared to say. I wasn't so sure if Daddy was correct in saying that she was confused, for Aunt Ruthie was laying down some pretty tense talk that began to stimulate even my nine-year-old youthful mind.

Wilma Troop and Aunt Ruthie sat at our bald four legged kitchen table while Daddy cleaned and gutted catfish. We didn't have much furniture in our housing unit, only the things that were necessary— a couch, a table and chairs for our wee kitchen, and beds to sleep in. The beds had been donated to us from a church organization. Aunt Ruthie's large full lips barely opened and her words dragged on as if she was talking in slow motion. "Only thang I's be full of is da trut'. See, Negroes don't like ta hear da trut' cuz da trut' hurts."

"Speak-it to da brother now!" Wilma added in her two cents.

"We don't need yo' weight in here now, you put yo' weight in here and somebody's liable to get crushed," remarked Daddy. Wilma Troop, feeling terribly insulted, removed her big body and went upstairs to talk to Mama.

"I jus' don't know but what my brother gots to be da biggest damn fool to waste his time wit' a woman like you. All dese intelligent, decent women in da world and dat fool gits stuck with you, I be damn!" Daddy shouted.

"I's give dat Negro what he wonts. I's give dat Negro what he needs. Futhermo' dis don't be 'bout me and my man dis be bout you sendin' dem damn kids over dere in Honkeyville. Look at 'em, all of 'em jus' 'bout got scars on 'em where dem crazy folks done jumped on 'em. Dose peoples don't wont us dere, dey ain't got no hearts fo' us. You mark my words, dose kids ain't gon fogit da hell you sendin' dem through. Talkin' bout yo' brother bein' a fool—hell you's da fool!" Aunt Ruthie hollered.

Daddy got so angry that he simply wanted Aunt Ruthie out of his sight. "Save yourself Ruthie, go lie down on the couch, kick yo' feet up and go ta sleep. Save yo'self!"

"You don't be tellin' me what ta do. You best be trying ta save yo' weak ass. You black and ain't no need of tryin' to be white 'cause you black and you cain't change. Bein' white you might as well be da slave of da devil. Das what dey all be anyway—demons."

Daddy didn't make me excuse myself from their presence even after they had started using vulgar language. From this I knew that Daddy was boiling mad. So mad that he had forgotten all about me sitting at the table across from Aunt Ruthie.

Daddy stepped away from the kitchen sink. He was holding a fish head in his hand. "What the hell you know about trying to be anything? Other than a bad sore for somebody's eyes." He slammed the fish head down into the plastic garbage bag. "What da hell you know about white folks? Ain't been around one enough ta know what dey breath smell like. I work with white folks almost every day. If it wan't for some white folks today, I wouldn't be able ta feed my family."

Aunt Ruthie had her pressed hair brushed back and matted down to her head. She could hardly hold her eyelids open. It seemed as though there were a couple of batteries in her brain that were slowly dying out. She continuously struggled to keep those batteries going, to keep her eyelids in the up position. I got so frustrated watching her that I wanted to take some sticks and use them to hold up her eyelids. Unlike a dead battery, Aunt Ruthie would all of a sudden recharge and blurt out something.

Mama came downstairs. Mama, shy and so much younger than Daddy, looked more like she could be Daddy's younger sister than his wife. One would think that after nine kids someone thirty-seven would look like ninety-seven. Not Mama. Always trying to keep peace on the home front, she attempted to divert the conversation. "Aunt Ruthie, why don't you come lie down on the couch. You be lookin' so tired."

"Yeah, ever since I done got dis thang called a job!"

Mama walked over to the sink beside Daddy. "Boy, this fish gon be for some good eatin' later."

"Aaaaay-man to dat!" Aunt Ruthie licked her lips.

Daddy walked into the pantry room and closed the grey curtain behind him.

"Been tryin' to teach yo' husband a little somethin' 'bout black pride. Gon tell me 'bout smellin' some honkey's breath. Wat da hell I wanna smell some white folk breath fo'? Fool don't even remember where he comes from, but cain't nothin' make me fo'git it. Yes sir, I knows where you comes from."

The grey curtains flung open. Daddy came out of the pantry. His half-full liquor bottle was wedged inside of his inner left elbow, held close to his body. He set his bottle and whiskey shot glass on the kitchen table and wiped his hands off on his white apron, which was splattered with fish blood. Daddy gulped down his first shot and looked over at Aunt Ruthie as she sat slouched in the chair with her head slightly lowered. He no longer looked at her with anger but with pity and shame. Aunt Ruthie had picked a soft spot. As he refilled his whiskey glass he said, "You ain't got no notion where I came from, lady." He gulped down his second shot. Aunt Ruthie didn't look up at his tall frame, didn't have enough charge to hold up her head.

Wilma Troop hollered down at Mama. "Sarah! Come 'ere girl and look at dis on da TV!" Without any hesitation Mama trotted upstairs.

Daddy slid out a chair from underneath the table and took a seat. Aunt Ruthie was sitting a couple of feet diagonally behind him and within his peripheral vision. Daddy fondled his whiskey glass. "What's a man to do? Must be like my old friend R.T. say, "Weeell I guess it depends on da woman," Daddy chuckled.

"Ha! You ain't jus' said nothin'. It be da same 'fo da woman, it depends on da man." Just for a moment Aunt Ruthie managed to lift up those eyelids.

"Ya know, that brother of mine you been seein' all dese years means the

3

world to me. Don't you thank I ain't got no mo'. Gots lots mo', jus' don't see 'em much. All our daddies be different, guess dat's just the way my mama was; guess she liked all different types, a little bit of dis a little bit of dat. I ain't never seen my daddy before, don't think I have. At least don't remember seein' him." Daddy poured himself another shot of whiskey, then slid the whiskey bottle to the center of the table as if he had poured his limit. As he swallowed he clenched his teeth together—his third shot seemed quite painful going down. A different man was emerging, a man I had seldom seen—and then only when Daddy was in the company of his whiskey glass. "Me and yo' man Cleo, my granmaw took care of us. Granmaw must of went crazy when dem white men killed our uncle. Yep, right down there in dem backwoods in Arkansas. Jus' 'cuz he looked at some white girl. Dey came and got 'im and we never saw his body again, nope we never did find his body. Every chance I could git I'd go and steal from da white man so I could take food home so my granmaw and us could eat. My granmaw sho nuff was crazy about me. I must have been about twelve years old when she died.

I took off, snuck on dem freight trains tryin' ta git north. I was a little hobo. Every chance I could get I stole from da white man, I got caught a many a-times too. Den I ended up in dat damn prison when I was thirteen. Yep I robbed dat white man and dey took my butt straight ta prison. I hid dat money on da inside of my belt; it was ninety-five dollars and a five dollar check. When dey stripped me down in prison dey found dat money in da lining of my belt. Dem grown men beat da shit outta me too. Only reason why dey didn't kill me is cuz I laid down on dat flo' and pretended like I was dead.

In a couple of years I got my parole and dis here white lady and her husband took me into they home. I labored my tail off for those people and every week when I was suppose ta git my pay dat ol' woman kept my money." Daddy stared into the whiskey bottle that was still in the center of the table. "Stole my money every time, her husband didn't like me talkin' bout he gon send me off ta 'form school. I didn't wonna go ta no damn 'form school.

I got my chance one day when I was up on they hill pickin' cotton. The governor's big fancy car pulled up alongside the road and I took off running down dat hill. The man that was sitting up on his horse keepin' watch on the cotton pickers started yellin'. He pointed his rifle at me. 'Where you goin' boy?! Get back here boy. Where you goin' boy?' 'I'm goin' ta see the governor, goin ta see the governor,' I yelled back. 'You git back here boy!' I ran up ta dat governor's car cryin', Mr. Governor sir, please help me, dey gon send me offta 'form school . . . please help me sir, dey done took all my money. The governor looked up at me, 'How many white men have you killed boy?' 'I ain't killed none sir.' 'You git in the back of my car you going with me.' That governor's wife took me in her kitchen and showed me my trade. She taught me everything I know. I was they cook and they number one chauffeur too. I drove da big man around everywhere he wanted ta go. I even tended their kids for them.

I remember, I was s'pose to be watchin' their little girl while she was playin', and dis old black fella dat worked on the land right next ta us said he would watch her while I took a nap in the shed. Old man Lester was a good man, don't know whatever happened to him. Da governor came out and saw his girl out there playing and he looked around and didn't see me. He came up in dat shed where I was nappin'. Kicked me all in the face with the heel of his boot. I was trying to explain ta him that Lester was watching her for me, blood was running all outta my nose and mouth but he jus' kept on kickin. I was his number one watchdog, I kept watch on all da black workers. Everythang they did I told. "Yes sir I saw 'em take it, he did it governor. Yes sir I heard him say it." His sad voice paused. The tears hid inside the glands of a body that was too much of a man and too much of a daddy to reveal them.

"Damn white men down south sho was somethin' else." 'Hey boy! Don't you know how ta say yessuh?' They'd grab me by my collar. 'Com'ere boy, don't you know how ta say yessuh? Say yessuh, boy! Dumb nigger ape don't know howta say yessuh.' Damn bastards! Sometimes I just wanted to gather a bunch of 'em up, take a machine gun and mow 'em all down. I stole from 'em every chance I could get. I ain't never killed nobody though," he sounded relieved. Daddy paused. "I tied one up, da white man I robbed and went ta prison fo'. I stuck 'im up and tied 'im up and kicked 'im in da butt. They never did find that pistol I used. I took dem to a pond and told dem dat I threw it in there. I didn't throw dat pistol in dat pond. I gave dat pistol away to a black man and he got rid of it for me."

Daddy went back to when he was working at the governor's. "When I ran away from the governor's so I could get north, dey came after me on dey horses, with dem damn dogs. 'Woof woof woof, a-boogadie boogadie boogadie. Woof woof woof, a-boogadie boogadie boogadie.' I found me a small tin can up in the woods, it was open on both ends. I took that can and ran down in da swamp. I sit down on the bottom of dat shallow swamp and tilted my head back. I stuck my nose just a little bit from underneath dat water and I breathed into that can. They didn't see me, dem dogs and horses ran right across that river. God! When my breath went into dat can and came back into me, I knew den dat I had a right. Dat I had a right ta be here and ta live like a man, like a real human being. I knew den dat there was somethin' wrong wit da way I had ta run and hide—bein chased down like some damn animal. 'Bout da way I stole and robbed so I could survive sometimes. See, when dey didn't catch me down there hidin' in dat water, I knew I had a mind—knowledge and the ability to think. And look at my kids, the same breath dat came back into me through that can, been passed on to all nine of 'em, that's right! Dey all mine too." He hesitated then his head slightly lowered. "Dey almost didn't come to be too, back when I was in that prison, listened to dat damn guard. I got a cold and I was a little bit sick, dat white guard told me ta put some penicillin down in my private and I would git better. He gave me somethin' in a needle. I injected it down into my thang. I been havin' pain ever since." Daddy's voice strengthed. "Bet dat fool rollin' over in his grave. Cuz I got nine and I made 'em all. Gon try my damndest ta make sure dat dey have a right ta go any place dey wanna go. That dey don't havta hide up in some little corner in this huge world, away from everybody and everythang. This world is too big ta take a seat in one corner. My kids gon know people whether dey be black or white. Some of dem folks been good and kind to me, and I jus havta try ta live by dat. I don't wont my kids ta beg and steal and rob, so when dey get caught somebody can walk up to them and kick dem in the face jus' because they wont to. My sons, I'm hopin' when my boys go out there and earn they pay they gon know what ta do so cain't nobody jus' take it away."

Daddy, surprised at Aunt Ruthie's silence, turned to look at her. His eyebrows lowered and his clenched lips relaxed a bit. He was angry that she had fallen asleep and not heard him. But relieved that she hadn't seen parts of his past, relieved that she hadn't seen some weak spots in his manly character. Aunt Ruthie had missed out, for this was a part of Daddy that was rarely revealed and she was not going to get a rain check.

Daddy turned back toward the whiskey bottle. "You ain't got no notion where I came from lady. Best believe though, I ain't gon forgit." Daddy knew that he was ashamed about where he had come from. He knew that he wouldn't forget—just didn't want to remember.

I didn't understand myself what it all really meant for him. But he was rarely so open about himself, his past, that I felt that Aunt Ruthie had missed out on something very important. Yep, those batteries in her head had finally died out. I wanted to replace them with new ones, to shake that booze out of her so she could wake up to hear all those things that Daddy had said.

Chapter 2

We were painting. There were deep blues and reds, pastel pinks and oranges. Newspaper shielded the classroom tables from paint spills. The colors overwhelmed me, the paint stunk. It had a smell that was unfamiliar to my nose, it was strong and it made my nostrils clog. I can remember running to the coat room, where my jacket was hanging. I could sense somewhat that if I took my jacket and headed for the door that I would probably be doing something wrong. I also had no idea how to get home. I left my jacket hanging and stood in the corner of the coat room crying.

My teacher and a few of the other kids followed me into the coat room. Ms. Mae Dilla was a tall, thin blond with short hair and round rim glasses. She knelt down beside me and asked what was wrong. I didn't know how to answer because I wasn't sure what was wrong myself. I just wanted to go home, so I kept whining. The other kids were staring at me. There was one girl in particular that stared at me with her shiny eyes as if she was thinking, "Why are you so unhappy? This is a fun time. You look so sad, I'll be your friend." Ms. Mae Dilla had a warm and bright smile and she kept on smiling at me. I started feeling guilty for requiring so much attention and for being the oddball.

I can remember this happening many more times. Each time Ms. Mae Dilla would hold my hand and guide me to a side door of the school building. Across the street from the school was the Teesmith Gardens housing project where I lived in a three bedroom unit with my parents and my four brothers and four sisters. From the side door our housing unit was visible. My teacher and I would wait to see a hand-waving figure come into view. After we got the signal, I would run across the street and meet my mother halfway.

When my older brothers and sisters came home from school, they would tease me as they were teased when they first started kindergarten. They'd sing, "Kin-der-garden ba-by al-ways cra-zy wal-kin down the street with a bald head-ed ba-by."

Going to kindergarten at a school where none of my other brothers or sisters went was quite traumatic for me. My patient and loving mother paved the road and made my journey a lot easier by often assuring me, "Don't worry, you only have ta go there for kindergarten. Then you will go ta school over the bridge with the rest. See their school don't have a kindergarten, they start with first grade. So dat's why you hafta go ta Dalbot."

I still dreaded going to Dalbot. If there was one thing I hated most about Dalbot public school, it was the sound of the school fire alarm. All students were forced from their classrooms and into the streets by the loud shrilling sound of bells. "Dong! dong! dong! dong!" The dongs were so loud and thunderous that my head couldn't contain the waves. The sound waves banged through my ears and leaked from my head into my body. It was as if we were all responding to some type of evil calling and something absolutely terrible was about to happen. There were no dings, like ding dong, only "Dong! dong! dong!" My ears had never heard such a thing. I was petrified and my limbs vibrated from fear. I wanted to run as far away from those bells as possible.

******

"At St. Anne's our fire drill don't sound like that. It sounds like this, bzzzz bzzzz," explained my older brother David as he pepped me up for my first day at St. Anne's Catholic school. Nothing worried me more than the thought of St. Anne's having a fire drill just like the one at Dalbot. I was indeed very relieved.

"You don't have to worry 'bout clothes cuz we have ta wear uniforms and white blouses," my sister, Sistine, who was in the third grade at St. Anne's told me. I wasn't all that thrilled or excited about the dress code change nor did I rebel against the idea. I just wanted to fit in with all the rest, for things to be simple, no drastic changes. Just let me go to school with my sisters and brothers and in this, I was sure, I would find enough excitement and contentment.

Daddy drove us to school on my first day. St. Anne's light yellow brick building was small in comparison to Dalbot's. As we exited from my daddy's station wagon, the giggling and chit-chattering partly ceased amongst the many groups of students that were standing in front of the school building. Sistine guided me over and unleashed me into a cluster of first graders. There were a couple of smiles and a few grimaces tossed my way. I knew no words, had no voice. A white statue of the Virgin Mary stood in the center of the school front lawn which was surrounded by a wire fence. I walked a couple of feet away from the cluster and leaned against the fence. I stuck my trembling brown fingers through an opening in the fence and clung to the wire. I could make the bodies of the boys, who were dressed up in dark blue pants and blue crossed ties, disappear. I could also fade out the brown checkered uniform dresses and white blouses that were just like mine. However, the stares from all those white faces were too overpowering. For the first time I could feel, what seemed to me now as a heavy mass, the layers of my brown skin from head to toe. My skin no longer appeared or felt clean. That wired fence became the quickest best friend that I have ever made.

Chapter 3

It was Chicago, nineteen seventy. The Beatles were still hot in America, the Vietnam War was moving along and civil rights leader Dr. Martin Luther King had been laid to rest. Because of slowly changing attitudes, it was also a moment when black folks were making mad dashes at newfound opportunity. For my parents it was like a gold rush in the sixties and early seventies. The Catholic Church and school had its arms open and my parents didn't hesitate to indulge in their welcome. My parents dreamed that their children could do and have better than they themselves had.

My two eldest sisters and oldest brother had been fortunate enough to complete St. Greg's Catholic Prep School. St. Greg's was about two blocks up the street from our housing complex. St. Greg's was demolished because of insufficient funding to rebuild the school. I had the opportunity to visit St. Greg's before it was torn down. My older sister, Letha, had to practice for an upcoming school benefit show so she took me to practice with her. She stood on a small platform along with a few of her classmates. They each held very colorful and long paper ribbons. Around and around the ribbons went as they whirled them in the open air and shook their hips to the beat of the music. They sang along with the music. "Cow-boys and In-di-an-an-ans oh oh oh oh oh oh. Cow-boys and In-di-an-an-ans oh oh oh oh oh oh." There was lots of laughter and their faces were full of smiles. I wanted so badly to be a part of it all. "You be starting school soon, before you know it you will do this stuff too," one of Letha's classmates told me.

St. Greg's school bus was sitting in the school lot and my brother Joseph and I were running to it. I dropped my Twinkie snack cake. The bus was about to pull off but someone saw us and the bus waited. Joseph was taking me along with him on his eighth grade school picnic. When we got on the bus his friends crowded around us. "Is this yo' sister?"

"Is this your little sister?"

"Is dat your sister?" There was laughter and some of the girls were pulling on my cheeks. "She is so cute."

"Yep isn't she?"

"She sho' is."

I wanted to be part of it all. St. Greg's had become like a lighthouse to our black community that surrounded it. It was like family. All types of sales and shows were organized in order to try and save the doomed school and church, but failed.

And so children and adults alike stood around and watched St. Greg's crumble to the ground. Their sad eyes wept and there became an empty space inside their hearts. I, along with my older siblings, Louis, David, and Sistine, and my younger brother and sister, had to accept our future prep school training at St. Anne's, for Daddy strictly wanted his children to attend Catholic school.

Chapter 4

When Daddy wasn't working on the railroad he'd always be more than happy to drive us to school, but for the most part, Daddy was always on the road so we usually had to walk. Louis, David, Sistine and I would walk two and a half blocks west to the opening of a two-block-long viaduct. At that point we met with Sareeda and Ricky, a brother and sister who attended school with us. Ricky was in the fifth grade and Sareeda was in the same grade as Sistine. We were the only two black families attending St. Anne's. Although a newcomer and in first grade, Ricky and Sareeda instantly accepted me as one of the gang. I suppose it had something to do with the fact that I was a clan member of the minority.

The viaduct was grim but never too dark for us to see our way to the other side. It was always partially lit by the sunlight peeking its way through both open ends. We trotted through the pigeon dump, old cans, bottles and dried-up smelly urine to the other end of the viaduct. Once we had made our way through the viaduct, there was definitely more silence among us than when we had entered. Fear overshadowed us, probably more in some than others. We had entered into the all-white Rodepoint community of mostly Irish and Polish ethnics. From this point we had to walk approximately seven-and-a-half more blocks before we reached St. Anne's. We were all aware that there were many in the Rodepoint community who forbade us to trod through their neighborhood. We were also aware that there was the possibility that we could meet with some disturbance before we reached school.

As we had many days before, we made our way without any confrontations. The sun shone brightly, for an early spring morning was upon us. There were still patches of smoothly formed snow on the sidewalks, the neighboring lawns and the school front lawn. The rays from the sun warmed the chilly air. The students formed clusters in front of the school building waiting for the school bell to ring. Most of my classmates had gotten used to seeing a brown face around, so I didn't feel too uncomfortable standing partially inside a cluster of co-first graders. There were a few hellos thrown my way but no one said anything else to me or tried to start a conversation. I swallowed my words and had no voice anyway. I removed myself and clung to my best friend. I am certain that my distance was noticed but no one ever seemed to hint any concern.

A little before the bell rang, a car pulled up in front of St. Anne's. Out popped blonde-haired Ms. Mae Dilla, my kindergarten teacher from Dalbot. It was easy for me to recognize that white face from my side of town. She smiled at me and it was that same bright, penetrating smile that she had always given to me in kindergarten. That smile went right through me, the chilled air became warmer and the sky seemed much brighter. She didn't speak, though she nodded her head to acknowledge my presence. What was Ms. Dilla doing visiting St. Anne's, I wondered to myself. I hoped that she was coming to St. Anne's to be my teacher; my grip on the wired fence loosened a bit.

In class we sat in a semicircle and took turns reading sentences from our Dick and Jane book. My turn came. "See Dick and Jane run. See Dick chase his dog Spot. 'Here Spot, here Spot,' Dick yelled." When I looked up to get approval from my teacher, I, as well as she, was taken by surprise. Mrs. Raydon had her brunette hair brushed back into a ponytail so her face stood out. She had a look on her face that seemed as though she had just seen Jesus Christ himself. Her eyes were wide and her mouth hung open. I think I had broken a barrier. Though I am sure that she thought that, regardless of my stigmatic skin color, I could do it and she wanted me to be able to do it; for she later constantly encouraged and motivated me. After just a few months in first grade, I was helping my brother spell and punctuate from his fourth grade spelling book.

Before bringing out our lunches we covered our desk with cloth. I used plastic because it was less expensive. I enjoyed lunchtime at St. Anne's sixty percent of the time and dreaded the other forty. The sixty percent was when my Mama made my lunch. The forty was when Daddy made my lunch and when I didn't have a lunch at all. Mama always wrapped my sandwiches in aluminum foil or saran wrap so they would stay fresh. Mama decorated my sandwiches with my favorite toppings and always cut them nicely into two halves. There would always be a couple of fingerprint marks left on the bread from where Mama had pressed to cut the sandwiches; this I always found rather sentimental.

On the other hand, Daddy had no class in sandwich-making whatsoever. Daddy would slap large chunks of meat, surrounded by fat, in between large pieces of lopsided bread. He added scarce toppings not worth ever revealing and he didn't cut his sandwiches. He would finish it off by rolling it in wax paper. Come lunchtime the bread was always hard and dry and it was difficult to hold onto because it kept falling apart. Daddy's sandwiches didn't look edible, so half the time I didn't eat them. But when I did, I stretched my neck to make sure that no one saw me when I tried to pick the slabs of fat from the sides of the meat. Of course I stood out in class like a sore thumb and everyone was curious anyway as to what the black girl was eating for lunch.

If I didn't have a lunch, it was probably because I had thrown Daddy's sandwich in the trash. On the days when I didn't bring a lunch, Mrs. Raydon would always ask out loud if anyone wanted to share their lunch with me. They didn't all answer at once. Whenever there was too long a time of silence after her asking, Mrs. Raydon would always turn to blue-eyed freckle-faced Tommy. "Tommy, would you like to share your lunch with Cindy today? She doesn't have a lunch." Tommy was always more than willing to share his lunches with me. The experience itself was humiliating and there were many times when I turned down Tommy's offer. But there were also many times when I accepted gratefully. This had been a rather good day, for Mama had made me a lunch. Bzzzzzzzz... uh oh, fire drill time, I acknowledged. We marched out into the back lot behind the school building. What a breeze—no banging, no doom, no fear. It was definitely different.

After school I was the first to arrive at our meeting spot. Then came my two perm-haired brothers. Louis and David had natural light brown hair with red streaks. With their olive skin and new perms, they both looked like they had come off some tropical island. Many times people had difficulty in distinguishing them from girls. Sistine had definitely gotten gypped during her genetic makeup process. Instead of receiving some type of balance, Sistine was overloaded with Mama's color and dabbed with Daddy's. Sistine turned out high yellow. Pissy Sissy was just one of the nicknames we gave her. Finally everyone showed and we headed home.

We were passing Fabia's candy store about half a block from school and Ricky got a sweet tooth. "Hey, let's stop in Fabia's."

"Yeah, I want some pretzels," I said.

If not for the big white sign hovering above the sidewalk, Fabia's could easily be mistaken for just a regular two flat apartment building.

"Ding-a-ling-a-ling, ding-a-ling-a-ling," the bells attached to the front door rang as we all passed through.

"Roof, roof, roof, roof, roof, roof."

Fabia lived in the back of her store. Whenever she wasn't tending up front, Nicky, her little French white poodle, kept watch. He was kept well-groomed and he wore a red bow on each ear. Fabia always left the door that separated the store from her apartment wide open. Nicky would stand behind the hitched small wooden gate and bark his head off until Fabia showed.

Columns of tiny red roses designed on white wallpaper covered the walls. All the goodies laid open in canisters that were neatly situated behind a long semicircular glass countertop. The sweet smell of candy filled our pleased nostrils. There was so much to choose from: taffy apples, gum drops, chocolate bars, chips, chewing gum, the selections were endless. Fabia unhitched the gate and came up front. Nicky followed close behind.

"Hi, Fabia."

"Hi, Fabia," Sistine followed.

"Hi, Fabia."

"Hi, Fabia."

Smiling Fabia responded in a soft and low voice. "Hello kids."

Fabia looked like she had been taking plenty of leisure with those sweets herself. She carried double chins and was only about five feet, two inches tall. Her hair was as white as snow and stood motionless in a tall puff, as if it were a wig on a headstand.

We peeked through the counter tops and made certain that we didn't lean on the spotless glass. After saying hello, Fabia never really made much conversation. She just stood there in her bulkiness and watched us make up our minds. Fabia never showed any expressions of objection to us, only curiosity. Although, her curiosity wasn't quite as obvious as Nicky's. Nicky stared at us acutely with his dark black eyes. It seemed as though he was picking up some type of electrical pulses from Fabia that made him aware that there was something different about us from the other kids who came into her store.

"May I have five orange slices, please?" Ricky requested.

"Dag, I knew you were going to get those. Don't you ever eat anything else?" Sareeda pouted and stared at him through her thick glasses.

Orange slices are chewy, jelly-like, sugar-coated candies that are shaped in the form of a fruit orange slice. Once we got outside Ricky shoved two slices into his mouth. Then with every down bite he parted his lips so we could all see, and grinded the slices between his front upper and lower rows of teeth. Ricky was a persistent tooth brusher. His pearly whites and bright pink gums stood out from his beautiful dark chocolate skin like the full moon in a midnight sky. The mass of jelly oozed in the slits between his teeth.

"Yuck, yuck, yuck, yuck, yuck!" Sistine blurted.

"Ugh, Ricky, man, dat's nasty," David added.

"What a toothache," Sareeda continued in the direction home.

Thrilled, I stood there and watched. Ricky eating his favorite candy was a moment when I felt that I was getting a free freak show. We continued on our way.

"You ever notice how Fabia looks just like her dog?" Louis asked humorously.

"Yep, all she needs is two little red bows on her ears," Sistine answered. We all chuckled.

"Mrs. Linda was on my case again today," he pushed out his bottom lip and lowered his voice. "David, Da-vid Rob-berts, I told you to leave double space between each sentence." He pulled his lip back in. "Her tongue is always sticking out in between her lips and every time she talks she starts coughing and spit flies all in my eye."

"Ugh!"

"I'll be so glad when I git outta her class."

"Did you get one of Daddy's sandwiches today?" Sistine asked David.

"Nope, I got Mama's."

"Me too." I added.

"He makes me sick when he fixes lunch, I was so embarrassed eating my lunch today." Sistine revealed.

"I just threw mine away," Louis included.

We all laughed. I was relieved in knowing that I wasn't the only one suffering the brown bag dilemma.

Just before the viaduct was a small warehouse. Occasionally two or three of us would stop in. Sometimes I would leave the group and go alone inside the warehouse, then I'd catch back up before they reached the viaduct. On this day I trampled alone over the cans of paint and wood beams. I worked my way around the stacked boxes and tall shelves. I knew that I would find him soon. I peeked around a corner and there he was, a middle-aged robust white man.

"Hi," I said.

He looked up at me. "Hi." As usual he didn't smile, he just looked at me.

"Bye," I said.

"Bye," he said.

I trampled my way out and caught up with the rest.

"Was he there today?" Ricky asked.

"Yep."

"Just said hi?"

"Yep."

"I'm not goin' in there anymore," Ricky vowed.

"Me too," said David.

A small alley separated a two story, red apartment building from the viaduct. After we came out of the viaduct we stood in front of the gate that surrounded the building's front yard.

"Someone better go up there and knock," Sistine said. "If we don't she's gonna think we don't like her."

"It's not my turn. I went last time," David backed away from the gate.

"I don't want none of them apples," Louis left the group and went into Phil's candy store next door.

The door cracked open and a skinny black wrinkled arm slung through. Sareeda picked the dented and bruised apples from the hand. After the door closed we saw the curtain in the front window move and we all waved.

The rest of us piled into Phil's store. Louis was standing over the cracked plastic counter. The crack was covered with tape. There were three boxes of candy inside. We also leaned over the counter and pretended that we were having a difficult time choosing.

"How's ya'll kids doin'?" Phil asked sullenly. His face sunk in and his crossed eyes bulged behind a pair of trifocals that rested on the tip of his black nose. It was early springtime and in Phil's store it felt like one hundred degrees. We picked out a few pieces of candy and gave Phil our pennies. Sometimes he took our money and sometimes he gave us the candy free. When we got outside we stuffed the stale candy into our pockets.

"God does it stink in that place." David said.

There was a moment of silence.

We were out of sight from the red building. "Squeash, splat, thunk!"

"A-ha! You missed me."

Ricky fired back. "Thunk, thunk!"

Louis dodged behind a parked car and David ran behind a streetlamp pole. Me, Sistine and Sareeda weaved in and out of their way.

"Pow!" The last apple sounded.

"Ow!" David held his forehead.

We burst into laughter. Our families separated and continued home. We never really joined Sareeda and Ricky after school or on weekends. Their mother was pretty strict so they usually stayed within their section of housing units.

Chapter 5

Unlike Rodepoint, all the residences in Teesmith looked the same. Every unit had the same type and color of windowpanes, the same front lawn and the same porch steps.

We got out of school earlier than our friends that attended public school. By the time our friends were let out of school it would be time for us to do our homework. Then we'd have dinner and go to bed. It was only on weekends that we mingled with our neighborhood friends.

Once in a while, I'd go over and wait on the corner to meet with some of my friends as they were let out of Dalbot. I'd go especially to see the policeman that directed traffic so that the students could cross the streets. He befriended us kids and gave us Officer Friendly coloring books. We called him Officer Friendly. He and Ms. Mae Dilla were the only two whites who were giving their services to Teesmith.

One early evening after school I overheard David in his bedroom whining. "What's the matter, David?" I asked.

"I don't know. I don't know how ta read these stupid words." He pointed to his fourth grade spelling book. "I'm so dumb, I'm havin' a test tomorrow and Mrs. Linda is going to kill me. I don't know what I'm gonna do, all those white kids be smarter than I am, my God," he hesitated, "look, can you say this word for me?" He pointed to a word in his book. There was a long column of words on the page. Each word had its phonetic spelling and accented syllable shown in parenthesis right next to it. The word he pointed to was bowdlerize. I started to pronounce. I didn't look at the word, I looked at the syllable that was shown in parentheses. "Boud · ler · iz." He tried to mock me. "Bo · er · iz, bo · er · iz."

"Boud · ler · iz, boud · ler · iz," I repeated.

"Bo · lar · lar · iz bo · la," he started over, "Bo · er · iz . . . aw shoot."

I noticed that David was looking at the word rather than the syllable that was in the parenthesis. "Here, look at these letters in da box." I placed my index finger inside the parenthesis. I moved my finger across the syllables. "Boud · ler · iz, boud · ler · iz." He too placed his finger inside the parenthesis. "Bod · lar, bo· la · iz . . . I can't do it."

"When o and u are together they sound like ow, not oh. Say ow like somethin' hurts you."

"Ow, ow ow."

"And when you say dis," I pointed to the iz. "Don't say *is*, say *eyes*," I pointed to his eye then mine. "Like your eye and my eye. The long line on top of the i means to stretch da sound, eye eye eye."

"Bou · ou · ou · bow · la · eyes. Ou, bow · la · eyes, bou · la · eyes."

I repeated the syllable again. "Boud · ler · iz, boud· ler · iz."

"I can't say it right!" David's eyes followed down the column of words. "How bout this one." The word was categorized.

"Kat · a · gor · ri, kat · a · gor · iz," I pronounced.

"Boy that's pretty good and you're only in da first grade. How do you do it?"

"It's easy. Kat · a · gor · iz."

"Kat · uh · gor · iz, kat · ug · gor · iz. I'm so stupid! I'm never gonna get it right."

I started feeling real uneasy being able to pronounce better than David could. It bothered me when he kept saying how dumb he was. It also bothered me that his words weren't perfect. I wanted so badly for him to spit those words out and make them sound just the way I had. By no means was David stupid, just extremely slow in catching on to the concept. Eventually he learned to say the words well enough to get him by Mrs. Linda.

Later that evening I went into my parents' bedroom. I sat across Daddy's lap while he watched the evening news. "Daddy, how come those people are screaming and yelling like that?"

"Well," he hesitated. "Be-cuz, I'll tell you why, cuz dey don't like black people and dey don't want them to live in their neighborhood."

I read to myself a couple of the signs that some white boys were holding up on TV. GO HOME NIGGERS, NO NIGGERS ALLOWED. "What's a nigger?"

"A nigger is a low down dirty person," Daddy explained.

A few people were holding up their middle fingers. I had already picked up the meaning of that gesture. "Why don't they like blacks?"

"Because our skin is dark and their jus'." He didn't finish what he was saying. I suppose the uproar on television seized his attention, or he had just decided to hold back on a vulgar word. I didn't ask anymore questions and Daddy remained silent. I felt really scared.

"Goddamit! You mean to tell me, you were gonna send her out looking like this!" yelled Daddy. That following morning Daddy and Mama were on their knees and I was standing in between them. They were inspecting my uniform and Daddy was real pissed at Mama when he saw a spot on my blouse. "That's the only one I could find for her, da other ones are all too big. I bleached dat one three times." Mama's head lowered. Mama was right. I had watched her dig frustratingly through a pile of shirts for fifteen minutes.

The ground was still a bit damp so Mama made me wear my boots. When I got to school I joined some other students on a large piece of carpet. I looked around to make sure that everyone else was concentrating on changing from their boots to their shoes. I quickly removed one boot. I made certain that I held onto the top of my pearly white sock which was folded over my toes. I didn't want anyone to see the patches in my sock. I quickly slipped my foot into my shoe. Then I made sure again before removing my other boot.

"Ok, this is the name of a dancer and a singer. The letters are:" My teacher proceeded to write on the blackboard: S M Y D S J. Whenever someone completed the word they were entitled to pick a candy bar from the plastic orange pumpkin that sat on the teacher's desk. Hands raised.

"Shelly!"

"Is there an I?" Shelly asked.

"Yes," Mrs. Raydon marked in the letter *I*. S M Y D *I* S

"Is there an O?"

"No." Hands waved frantically in the air.

"Tommy!"

"A."

S*A* MY D*A* IS J. Quickly Shelly raised her hand. Her long blond hair swayed along with the movement of her hands. "Ooooh I know I know who it is." No one else had their hand raised.

"Ok Shelly."

"It's that nig-ger guy." She swallowed, "uh, uh."

"Shelly," Mrs. Raydon called in a low voice. Blood rushed to my face. My teacher moved her eyes back and forth at Shelly and me. Being reinforced that she had said something inappropriate, Shelly retracted herself. "Oh, I'm sorry; I mean that black guy, Sammy Davis, Jr." My eyes watered, to me black and nigger had the same meaning.

A few weeks later Shelly invited me to her birthday party. Shelly had been friendly and polite to me before what she had said in class and after, so I gratefully accepted her invitation.

That Saturday afternoon, Daddy drove me over to Rodepoint to Shelly's house. What a house I thought as I looked around at the new looking furniture, nick nacks and large mirrors that decorated the walls.

After we ate, Shelly's older sister told us to go downstairs in the basement and play. We all took off running and giggling behind one another. All of a sudden three of my classmates ran past me screaming and chuckling.

"Run quick."

"Here she comes."

"Don't let her touch you, you're going to catch it."

I slowed my pace but I didn't react emotionally to what they said. I was too busy admiring the carpeting on the steps and the wood banister on the staircase that led to the basement. The basement seemed like another house to me. There was new looking furniture there too, wall-to-wall carpeting and paneled walls.

I joined a circle that had formed around Shelly's four-year-old baby sister. She was kneeling over a coloring book. On the front cover of the coloring book were four black characters from a Saturday morning cartoon show. "Say nigger," someone whispered. "Say big lips."

"Ne-gur, ne-gur, big leeps, big lips," she said loudly placing her finger on the face of one of the characters. Laughter broke out. Realizing that she could make everyone laugh by doing what she was instructed to do, she repeated the practice, then she broke into giggles. I didn't know whether to laugh or cry. Shelly's older sister came downstairs and realized what was happening. "Shelly don't do that. That's not nice." Her big sister looked over at me. My eyes watered. She then retreated back upstairs.

"Go ahead Tommy, hold her hand."

"Yeah, hold it and catch it!"

"Hold her hand, I dare you."

They teasingly pushed and shoved him. I suppose this was Tommy's punishment for always sharing his lunches with me. I suppose this was his test to prove how much he really did like that black girl.

"Do it Tommy!"

"Yeah we dare you!"

They all laughed in a very silly way. Their plain, loud pink and blue party dresses made me feel empty inside. The dresses had no design, they were just there with no feeling to them. Tommy bashfully smiled at them as he tried to pull himself out of their way. He didn't look at me, I guess he didn't want to see the hope in my eyes. Would he do what they were telling him to do? Would he make them see that there was nothing abnormal about me? Tommy moved quickly to the other side of the room. My chest drew inward, my upper body was in pain. They had drawn a divider between Tommy and me. On the other side of that line, I saw myself being allowed to reach over only to accept part of Tommy's lunch. It was confirmed now: I was not one of them. I had it and whatever it was they didn't want to catch it; even Tommy had acknowledged this. Why had they made him choose between me and the other side of the room. I sensed that if Tommy and I had been alone, that just maybe he would have had no hesitation with holding my hand. But now he knew I had it, and so the divider had been created. I was hurting but I knew that it was not because of Tommy. . . .

"Ugh, uh, yuk!." I lifted up the concrete-like bread. Where was the meat? I thought. There was nothing but a big slab of fat. "Fat! fat! fat!, Daddy did it again."

"Tommy, Cindy doesn't have a lunch today, would you like to share your lunch with her?"

"Yes." Tommy looked into my eyes. He had been full of the same compassion so many times before. I knew that he knew that I had it. Therefore, I never saw the possibility of anything more ever happening between us, other than the sharing of half a sandwich.

Chapter 6

A new family moved in a couple of doors down from where I lived, so I went over to see if there were any girls my age to play with. Ruby Mae was a little older than I was but she was very friendly and we started a conversation. After we had found out a few things about one another Ruby Mae asked, "Why you be talkin' like dat?"

"Like what?" I responded stupidly.

"You know, through your nose."

"What, through my nose? I talk through my nose?"

"Yeah, and all proper and stuff, jus' like a honky."

I felt embarrassed. To defend myself I explained, "Well see, I go ta school with white kids over in the white neighborhood," I swallowed and tried to take control of my voice and alter my tone, "and I guess it jus' be wearin' off on me."

"I hate when you be talkin' like dat it be soundin' phoney. How many brothers and sisters you got?"

As I counted, I took my right index finger and placed it on the tips of the fingers on my left hand. I told her the names of all my sisters and brothers. I was certain to give her the nicknames that we used in our neighborhood. "Pepe (Letha), Broomhead (Louis), Too-Too (David), Moosey (Sistine)..."

Ruby Mae turned out to be perfect for the talent shows that we held mostly on Friday nights. There was a basement underneath our row of housing units. There were six units on a row. The basement continued from one end of the row to the next. A couple of washing sinks and water pipes for laundry lined the concrete walls in the basement. On the opposite side of the sinks were a row of laundry rooms, one room per housing unit. Each room had its own lockable gate, but the enter/exit gates were usually left open. The laundry rooms looked like individual jail cells. My parents were in charge of the access to the basement. On the Fridays when Daddy, who forbid us to play in the basement, was out of town we were always able to convince Mama to give us the keys.

The space between the laundry rooms and the sinks was our stage for the talent shows. We usually practiced one hour before the show. The boys prepared their impersonations of the singing groups the Temptations, the O'Jays and James Brown. The girls usually imitated the Supremes and although they were an all-male group, the Jackson Five.

Ruby Mae wore her hair really wild, like all over the place. She was so thin, if anyone had ever held her upside down by her feet, she would have made the perfect mop, stick and all. With her dashing smile and big round eyes she looked just like one of the Supremes. Without first having to audition her voice, Ruby Mae gladly accepted the vocal lead in our Supremes act.

Moosey swung her hips in one direction and moved her arms in another. "Look, if we sweep out dis way it ain't gonna look right. Cindy, go sit over there and tell us how dis looks." I leaned against one of the washing sinks and watched while Moosey, Ruby Mae and Kathy took their positions. Kathy was nine years old like Ruby Mae. Kathy had a wonderful voice but she was an awful dancer. She was so stiff and whenever they moved she was always three steps behind. "It looks alright. Ya'll better come on, we only have fifteen minutes left and we have to do the J-five routine." My little sister Anita and her friend Tina ran around us playing and acting silly. Tina put her hands on her waist. "Uh-uh ya'll ain't gone win, dat looks stupid." We chased them out of the basement.

"But I don't wanna play the bongos—I wanna sing." I wanted a change of pace.

"Nope, I'm Michael," assured Kathy.

"That's no fair! You and Moosey always do Michael and I never get a chance."

Kathy pivoted her head from side to side. "Cuz you cain't sang!" She was only reminding me of my terrible singing ability. Ruby Mae and Moosey dropped to their knees laughing. I laughed along because I knew it was true. All the other girls had wonderful singing voices. I was the better dancer and bongo player.

We had popcorn, soda pop and candy for refreshments. We charged ten cents for admission. I never received any objections from the other kids for being a girl and tapping away on my brother's bongos. "Rap tap tap pa-pop a boom boom. Rap tap tap pa-pop a boom boom." I knew I was getting down because everyone's head was moving to the beat. The kids that were leaning up against the walls and sitting on the concrete floor cheered and applauded.

The copycat Temptations excited the crowd. They snapped their fingers, spun around, dropped to their knees and bounced back up singing, "Pa-pa was a rol-lin stone doo doo doo . . ."

Our show ended and squarehead Freddy Brown, Broomhead's best friend, won for his Elvis Presley routine which he always did so well. Like most, I could spend hours in awe just watching Freddy wiggle his pelvis and sing Presley love songs. Unlike Elvis, Freddy was very muscular and large-boned but he was just as good.

"Ya'll I got blisters on my hand from beatin' them bongos so hard."

"Come on Freddy, wiggle us some Presley again, jus one mo' time. Show us yo' stuff."

"Man, ya'll need ta cut out dat boppin' stuff cuz it ain't even workin'. My mama can bop better den ya'll."

"Yo' mama is a bop."

"Hey man, don't be talkin' bout my mama!"

I could never have fun like this with the kids at school. Bet they would never imagine that I sing and dance and play bongos, I thought. Sure they wouldn't wanna know; we're just too different, that's all.

Who was it going to be? Who was going to be this week's victim as our talent show had come to its end? I prayed that their eyes would not find me for I hated dark places, I especially hated being in dark places alone. Once in a while they'd do it to one of the girls but their usual prey was a boy. If they couldn't come up with a lure they'd use force to get the person inside, then they would lock the laundry room gate. They'd fill the mind of the captured person with tons of scary thoughts. Then they'd turn off the lights and vacate the basement. I certainly did not want to be the one left behind inside that laundry room.

I believed that there was a devil that had five-feet-tall horns on his head, fangs and a winded up old face. Many times before when I had done mischievous deeds, my sister Pepe had promised me that if I didn't admit my wrongdoings, I would receive a visit by something in the night that would scare the living hell out of me.

Pepe was in high school already. When she was about four years old my brother Joseph threw a lighted match into her hair. Mama put the flames out using her own bare hands. Pepe's hair was extremely short, it was hard to believe that it had once hung below her shoulders. A lot of older men were very attracted to her. Daddy had lost a couple of friends because they had made flirtatious comments about her. This was a rather ironic thing for Pepe looked like a boy and tried to do most everything boys did. She was secretly dating this one older man only because he gave her free lessons on how to ride his motorcycle. Give Pepe a baseball glove or horror movie and she would feel like she was on top of the world.

A local newspaper had run a series of creature photographs and Pepe posted them on our bedroom wall. She had me convinced that those creatures came down off that wall at night. So I believed in ghosts too, the walking of the living dead. I remember that time when:

"Who ate my candy bar? Maama!" Pepe called. "Somebody ate my candy, it was in here in da freezer right on top of da ice tray. Ooooh," she whined. "Who ate my candy?"

"Dag! How come she had to come when I was down ta my last bite?" I hid resting on my knees in the small pantry that was right around the corner from our refrigerator. My tiny mouth gobbled up the rest. "She wan't gon git none of dis chocolate, uh-uh, it was too good ta give somebody some." Sometime that day I eventually stepped into her path. "Cindy, did you take my candy bar? It was in da freezer right on top of da ice tray."

"Naw," I answered guiltily. I was not a good liar, my conscience was an incredibly weak one. Pepe's instinct picked up on it right away. "Let's go, we're going up to the bathroom." She grabbed my hand and led me upstairs. She pushed me inside the bathroom and stood between the half-closed door. "Now when I turn off dese lights and close this door if you tellin' the truth ain't nothing gon happen, but if you be lyin' Mary Worth gon come out dat mirror. She has long, real long claws and a real big mouth wit teeth dat hang down to her chin. Her hair is all wild and she got big red holes in her face. She gon scratch out yo' eyeballs and eat your heart. I mo' tell you, she one mean lookin' heifer. Ain't nobody gon hear your screams, neither."

I confessed in a flash. I would have thrown that candy bar back up piece by piece if she had ordered me to. "Anythang! Anythang! Just don't close dat door."

Anyhow, I knew that I was too fragile for such an ordeal. After our audience had cleared, the older boys, the ten, eleven, and twelve-year-olds who had been part of the talent show, centered on Freddy's little brother. Freddy was in on it, too. Wooo boy, I sighed with relief.

"Hey Franco, you know dat wine-ol' Pooter? He was in here dis mornin' drunk and he crawled up over dere in dat corner and dropped a whole lotta quarters. Let's go in dere and see if we can find some."

Franco was around the same age as I, six or seven, and was square headed just like his big brother. Not knowing any better, the already jubilant Franco rushed that square straight into the laundry room; he wanted to be the first to get to the treasure. "Slam! lock." That square emerged from out of that corner so fast that time didn't get the opportunity to change. Franco leaned against the locked gate with his arms raised as if he was being frisked by a cop. "Naw, naw, please ya'll, please don't leave me in here." Franco was on the edge of diving over into a sea of tears. "Freddy I'm tellin' Mama, ya'll please, come on please."

"Last night Ms. Washington was down here washin' and she said she turned around and saw Daryl Dawkins standin' over dere foldin' up his clothes."

"You know he been dead fo' ten years!"

"When dem spirits come, boy, ya better sang cuz dey like dat funky music, and das da only thang dat gon keep dem offa you."

Franco shook the bolted gate wildly. "Maaamaaa, Maaamaa, help! I'm tellin' Freddy, I'm tellin'!"

"Oh yeah, if you hear some chains draggin', dat be dead Mr. Curtis, dat evil man dat use to live next dough to ya'll, he be washin' his clothes down here too."

"Aha, Francos gonna git spooked!" We taunted and scared little Franco up pretty good. I didn't say too much because I was thinking about who they were going to get next time. I sure was glad that I wasn't in Franco's shoes, standing behind that gate, begging for mercy from a bunch of thrilled pitiless pranksters.

We grabbed our things and headed out the door. We turned out the dim lights and closed the door behind us. The basement was full of nothing but darkness, dust and Franco's screams. "Ahhhhh ahhhhh Mamaaa, Maaamaaa!" We gathered on the set of steps that led to higher ground from the basement. Most held their aching bellies while they hysterically laughed. I only chuckled for I was still thinking about who they were going to get next time.

After about five or ten minutes Freddy went to release his little brother. When Franco stepped under the night light that was above the basement door, he looked away from our faces with embarrassment. The crotch and inner pants leg of his multi-patched overalls were soaked with warm urine. I think that Franco believed in the devil and the walking dead like I did. I had held back before but the sight of those pissy pants cracked me up. Snot flowed from his nose and into his mouth. He smiled sparingly and we knew that he was still with us, that he understood that it was all just a big joke. Even after all he had been through, he still had to suffer by being the victim of taunting.

"Uh-h, look, he peed on hisself."

"Ha ha ha ha."

"Uh-h, you nasty thang!"

Franco retreated to his front porch and let his last remaining tears flow. There was nothing else he could do. The boys who had initiated the prank were all too big for him to seek out revenge. If he went and told his Mama she would have just told him to, "Stop being such a cry baby boy, wipe dem tears from yo' eyes and go out dere and learn how ta be a big boy." Franco's last tears were by no means sad tears, they were glad tears, glad tears because we had finally let him out of that darn basement.

The next Friday when my Daddy would be out of town, we would all be at it again. As if God had sent down an electrical charge, one of us would get struck and that charge would transmit through each and every one of us. Our joints popped, jerked and glided to the rhythmic sound waves. Few people knew we existed, though we carried on like we were performing for the world.

Chapter 7

"Tomorrow we have ta find another route to take home," David said seriously as we paced in the direction towards home. "This guy in my class said dat a white gang was going to beat us up."

"I heard that too," Sareeda added.

We quickened up our pace. Louis had stayed home with a stomach ache. My heart skipped a beat, I felt more scared having one less person in our group. I hoped that my big brother would be well enough to come to school the next day.

"I think I know another way home," Ricky said.

In the shadow of what was supposed to occur to us, we made no stops anywhere until we got on the other side of the viaduct in our neighborhood.

All that next day while in class I worried. We had figured out another route but we didn't know if it was any safer than our original route. It helped knowing that Louis had come to school.

We were waiting for a longer time than usual for Louis to show up at our meeting spot. Ricky ran back inside school and found out from one of Louis' sixth grade teachers, that he had left for home earlier because of illness.

My legs trembled so much that each step became more difficult. I felt like I was walking and wasn't getting anywhere. I wanted to pick up my feet and fly away.

"How much further do we have ta go? My feet are burning," Sistine frowned.

"Just keep on walking." David took a quick glance behind us. We had already walked twenty minutes longer than we usually walked going home. We finally got to a busy street where there was heavy traffic. "Ha ha. Suckers got suckered this time," Ricky showed his pearly whites. "Guess we showed them."

"Bet they were just bluffing," said David.

"Look, look!" I shouted. There were two white boys a few blocks behind us. They were walking slow and looking into another direction. It was no worry. Even if they were after us they couldn't have caught us, we were too close to home. I must have startled Sareeda because she lashed out at me, "My God! You're so paranoid."

When we arrived home Pepe was standing in the front door. "Guess what? Louis is in the hospital."

"What happened?"

"Was coming home from school, some boys jumped on him and beat 'im up. Mama took a taxi ta go get him."

We had told Louis about the threat. Since he was leaving for home early he figured that he wouldn't have any problems taking the regular route.

Louis' hand partially covered the big white bandage underneath his eye. "Chumps too chicken to fight out in the open, they pulled me over a fence in somebody's backyard." The slamming shovel left a gash in Louis' upper right cheek that required twenty-one stitches. The scar from the wound never fully healed; it became a permanent member of his facial features. Every other week there would be another threat, and we often had to use our shortcuts to get home.

******

"Knock knock knock knock."

Broomhead answered the door.

"Hey man, ya'll father home?" Freddy whispered.

"Naw man come on in. My old man in New York."

"Dem white boys got me man."

"Ga-damn man dey mess yo' mug up. Yo' old man is crazy sending ya'll ta school in dat neighborhood. Hey man who dat yo' father hollin' at yesterday? He was kickin' somebody's butt."

"Oh that was Cindy gettin' a whippin'."

"Man we was sittin' way on Dennis' porch and we could hear him yellin', man we was bussin' up. Yo' old man is a trip."

"Knock knock knock. Ya'll father home?"

"Naw, come on in."

Once it got around that Daddy wasn't home our friends started piling into our small living room.

"Knock knock. Ya'll Daddy dere?"

"Nope, come on in."

There was Kathy, Freddy, Ruby Mae, Caesar, Dennis, Travane and Michael. All found a spot to sit so we could shoot the gossip.

"Let's practice fo' da talent shows," Caesar suggested.

"Nope, nope, we said we was gon practice first," Ruby Mae pouted. "Ya'll gon over Dennis house and practice, girls go first."

Caesar picked at his cropped Afro. "Ya'll jus' wait, when we git famous we gon be called da Magical Imperials and we gon have chicks hanging all over us. Ya'll jus' wait, den ya'll gon wish ya'll was our slaves."

"Hee hee hee."

"Yeah, right!" Kathy said.

"What happened ta yo' face Broomhead?" Ruby Mae asked.

"Some white boys did it." Broomhead patted the bandage.

"Dem hunkies be crazy, I wouldn't be goin' ta school wit dem if I was ya'll." Ruby Mae said.

"Well you ain't dem so why don't you jus' shut up, bubble eyes," Dennis responded.

"You don't be callin' her no bubble eyes!" Kathy shouted.

"Yeah, don't be callin' me no bubble eyes."

"Ya'll I swear fo' swear da other day man, Michael ain't dis true?"

"Yep man, straight up."

Caesar continued, "Me and Michael went under dat viaduct over dere lookin' fo' some pop bottles. I told Michael 'ya'll, yu goin' too far.' He talking bout 'Naw man, naw I wonna git some mo bottles cuz I wonna git that box of cereal.'"

Michael laughed. "Man you ain't gotta be tellin' 'em all dat, just tell 'em what happened."

"He started walking ta da other side and my stupid self listened ta 'im and followed right behind him. When we got on da other side in dat place—what they call it? Rod Ronpote, it was dis parked car over dere full of white boys. Dis white boy jumped out and said, "Come ere you nigger boys." Man, I dropped dem damn bottles and took off like a hawk. Two mo jumped outta da back seat and came after us wit chains and bricks, one dude had a ax."

"Uh-uh, you be lyin' dey didn't have no ax. Dey jus had some chains and stuff."

"Michael wit his stupid self, tried ta run wit all dem damn pop bottles! Man I didn't care—I was gone."

We all laughed.

"No I didn't, I dropped 'em."

"Dat be why you had fo' of dem when we got back to da other side?"

"Ahhhhh!"

"Ha ha ha."

"I don't know how ya'll be doin' it. Don't ya'll be scared?" Caesar asked.

Broomhead stared down at the floor. "Hecky yeah, hecky yeah man!"

I hated hearing my big brother say he was scared. My inner fears became magnified. I went upstairs and got my brother's bongos. "Rap-ta-rap rap rap, rap pop pop a pop. Rap-ta-tap rap-tap tap, boom boom boom boom, rap tap tap a pop a boom."

"Hey now."

"Git down Cindy," Freddy yelled.

"Rap tap tap a pop a boom boom."

Hands came together. "Clap clap clap, clap clap clap!"

"Boom boom boom a boom a boom boom, a boom a boom boom. Boom!"

"Clap!"

"Boom!"

"Clap!"

"Boom a boom!"

"Clap! clap!"

My bashful side crept in. "Ya'll, I'm takin' a break . . . my hands be hurtin'."

"Aw come on Cindy."

"God lee!"

"We was just gittin in da beat."

The three Magical Imperials took over. Freddy stepped forward to sing the lead while Dennis and Caesar stood behind him doing their fancy dance steps. "Money money money mon-neee."

Caesar and Dennis added from the background, "Moneeeeee."

"Money money money mon-neeeee."

"Moneeeee.

"Some people got ta have it, yeah. Some peoples really need it, yeah. Do dangs do dangs do dangs bad dangs wif it, yeah. Do dangs do dangs good dangs wif it. Money money money, mon-neee!"

"Mon-neeee!"

"Some peoples got ta have it, yeah. Do dangs do dangs bad dangs, do dangs do dangs do dangs good dangs wif it, yeah!"

Snapping their fingers they switched to another tune. "Doooo snap! Doo doo doo doo snap! Doooo snap! Doo doo doo doo snap!" Again Freddy sang the lead, "I got sunshine on a clou-dy day. When it's cold outside I got da month of Maaaay. What-can-make-me-feel-dis-way? My girl, my girl, talking bout my girrrl."

"My girl!"

"Yeah!"

"Alright Imperials."

Ruby Mae took to the floor. "Whenever you're wit me, I hear a syn-pho-neee."

"Sang it Bubble Eyes!"

Chapter 8

"Anybody want da rest of dese french fries?" Freddy Brown held up a brown paper bag with grease spots all over it. Me, Freddy's little twin brothers and a group of other kids were hanging around the neighborhood telling jokes and playing games.

"Yeah!"

"Yeah. I want 'em."

"Ooooh, give 'em ta me Freddy."

"Here, ya'll share." Freddy handed over the greasy delectables that were smothered with ketchup. We passed the bag around.

"Hey Freddy, how come every time I see you, you always got a lotta money?"

"Yeah Freddy, where you be gittin' all dis money from?" Franco inquired.

"Wipin' car windows over at Lion's Park. Shaun, Broomhead, Caesar, Michael and Too-Too up dere now. I already made enough money fo' today so I came home." Freddy walked away with a dirty cloth hanging and flip-flopping out of his back pants pocket.

"What a good idea!" I thought. For most of the kids that I knew in the projects, including myself, receiving allowance money was unheard of. By the time Daddy finished paying the bills, there was no money left for luxuries. Twinkie cakes and Sayo chocolate milk, things that I wanted to add to my school lunches, were definitely considered luxuries in my household.

The time was perfect. It was Saturday evening, Mama was napping and Daddy was out of town. I asked Ruby Mae if she wanted to go up to Lion's Park and wash some windows. She was too chicken. Franco and some other kids my age were heading up that way so I excitedly joined their small crowd. I was the only girl in our wiping group. The boys didn't care and neither did I. Making fast money interested me more than jumping rope and playing hopscotch. Besides, I was already in the second grade and I felt I had matured enough for more exciting and new things. We were all a lot younger than the older boys who wiped windows, but we figured if they could do it, we could do it too. We got our wiping rags and headed off to Lions Park which was three-and-a-half blocks north of Teesmith.

Lions Park was the home of the Chicago Lion's baseball team. The baseball game and the entrance to the Walker expressway were the only reasons most white people had for coming over to our side of the viaduct.

Baseball season had just started. Two blocks away and we could already hear the roaring from the crowd that was inside the ballpark.

"Uh oh, somebody must of hit a home run."

Souvenir and food vendors occupied the street corners around the park.

"Hot dog! Get your hot dog! Get your hot dog, right here!"

"Shirts, one dollar man, jus' one dollar brother man."

"Gloves, your team caps, shirts, you name it we got it!"

Seven or eight parking lots surrounded the huge white, round, structure. Some were much larger than others. The big boys had already planted themselves on the larger lots so we found ourselves a small lot and split into two's. People started exiting from the ballpark at about 10:00, as early as the seventh inning. The seventh inning is two innings before the last inning, unless there was a tie after the ninth which could send the game into extra innings.

As the people approached their cars, I patiently waited until they got inside and closed their doors. Then, using my cloth, I grazed the front and side windows on the driver's side. I wiped lightly because my cloth was dry. If I had done otherwise, I wouldn't have done anything but smeared the dust on the windows. The white man smiled, gave me a dime and politely said thank you. I was in business. As we moved from car to car some people gave and some didn't. A lot of people just looked at us like we were crazy.

The lot had pretty much emptied except for a couple of cars. Me and Franco were about to leave when four white men approached one of the cars that was still sitting on the lot. Franco wanted to wipe their windows but I didn't want to because the men were laughing and talking real loud. They were leaning on one another for support, like they had had too much liquor.

"I'm not doing theirs, they may try something." I stepped back towards the direction we were heading in. Franco hesitated for a moment, then he ran that squarehead right over to the car.

"Hey fellas, looka what we got here."

He hesitantly wiped at their front window. I felt stupid when I saw them reach into their pockets and give him money. Franco excitedly came running back holding out his hand. "Look, look what I got." In the palm of his hand were four shiny half dollars. I felt even more stupid.

We headed off to meet with the rest of our group at R.C. Barbecue Joint which was right across the street from the park. The twenty-five cent pair of shoes that I wore didn't protect my feet any from the large and small pebble paved parking lots. The uneven gravel contorted the paperlike soles. My mind wasn't sure if it was daytime or nighttime. My aching feet kept telling me that it had been a long day, that it was time to check in. All the traffic so late at night, the blowing of the horns, the yelling, confused my brain. The super bright lights from the stadium only added to the illusion. There was way too much going on in order for me to comfortably think about sleep. My tired feet and body wanted silence.

When we got to the joint the big boys were there too. So this is where the hangout is after an evening's work at the ball game. I was kind of baffled. There were a few white people that had stopped in R.C.'s. The kids at school sometimes made fun of, and turned their noses away from, the sandwiches that I brought to school—even at Mama's nice sandwiches. I didn't think that white people cared for black people food like fried chicken and barbecue. The NIGGER GO HOME signs didn't have "P.S. But leave us some soul food."

"Oooooh, look man, yo' little sister is up here."

"Cindy, who are you up here with?" Broomhead asked.

"Them," I said pointing at the kids I had come with.

"Be careful and don't you get into anyone's car."

"I know how to run," I said proudly.

"How much money did you make?"

I showed him my sixty cents.

There weren't any seats in the joint so we just stood around. The smell of that soul food convinced my feet that they were being supported by a quality pair of one-hundred dollar shoes. The unleveled floor was chipping away and cracked in certain spots. Two workers fixed the food behind a large plastic window. While we waited for our various barbecue rib, chicken and french fry orders to be fixed, I listened while the boys talked.

"How much did you make?"

"Twenty-five dollars."

"I only made sixteen. Dats cuz Michael be takin' some of my cars."

"Uh un!"

"Dis lady gave me a five dollar bill."

"One dude tried to run me over; he said, "Git da hell away from my car, you scum." If I hadn't of moved outta his way, dat would of been it."

"Ha ha ha ha ha."

"Hee hee hee hee."

"Hey man, dat ain't funny, I could be dead."

"Ha ha hee hee hee."

I was disappointed when I realized I had made the least money. Though, I was glad that my big brothers had done well because they paid for my barbecue! Midnight was fast approaching so we all headed back home. Mama was real relieved to see me in the company of Broomhead and Too-Too. We sat on the front porch underneath the stars and watched Freddy wiggle his way in and out of Elvis Presley tunes. The spicy and sweet barbecue sauce had soaked into my taste buds. I savored the flavor. What a most memorable and wonderful moment! We bobbed our heads for about an hour until our eyes became heavy.

I became addicted to window wiping. When Daddy was out of town and Mama allowed me to go outside and play, I'd slip off to the ballpark. I got so determined that if I couldn't find anyone to go with, I'd hike the three-and-a-half blocks to the park alone. Too young and bold I was, in such an unpredictable world. I am certain that Mama and Daddy's prayers were in God's favor.

I became familiar with the area around the park, the restaurants, the gas stations, the vendors. I also made friends with some of the ushers that guarded the entrance/exit gates to the park. Around the end of the sixth inning the ushers would sometimes let us project kids in for free. Just like the other kids, I quickly learned my way around the inside of the park. I knew the location of every restroom facility, every up/down ramp for walking and every seating stand. Of course, I never really watched the game, just ran about the park looking for something to get into.

Pepe loved playing a baseball game with Freddy called strike-outs. Whenever Pepe managed to get tickets to the Lion's game, she would sit still through the complete game wearing a baseball glove on her hand. I would always leave her sitting and go on my journey through the park. I thought she was a bizarre individual who had no idea what fun was all about.

Chapter 9

"Here you go, take this." Daddy handed me a large box of candy. "And you know what I want you to do with it, don't you?"

"Yes, Daddy."

"What?"

"Share it?"

"That's right. Now take it outside with your friends and share. Make sure everybody gits some and don't be stingy."

"OK Daddy, thanks Daddy."

"Uh huh."

Daddy was a tall and husky man of fifty-three years. He stood tough like he was always on guard, just in case someone trespassed him. As long as no one encroached, his insides were as soft as marshmallow. I took the candy outside and some of my friends crowded around me.

"Oooh wee."

"Ooooh."

"Candy ya'll!"

Their small fingers searched inside the box. The candy went pretty fast. Ruby Mae and I sat alone on her front porch as she held on to the empty box. Ruby Mae came from a pretty big family too, although she didn't have a daddy. He took off and left her Mama with seven kids. Their two bedroom unit didn't have much furniture, and Ruby Mae had to sleep on a mattress on the living room floor.

"Boy, dis be a pretty big box of candy. It's real good too. Ya'll mus be rich, huh?"

I knew we struggled to make ends meet but I enjoyed feeling like I was on a pedestal. "My Dad told me not to tell."

"I wish my Mom could git me a box of candy dat be like dis. Can I keep dis box?"

"Nope." I took the box back.

"You be still talkin' like a honky!"

"No I don't."

"You do!"

I didn't like being around Ruby Mae too much. She always had to comment on the way I talked. "Forgit you Ruby Mae. I can't help it if my dialect bounces back and forth from one side of the viaduct to the other."

******

"This one here is twenty dollars and this one is thirty-five dollars." The white salesman told Daddy.

"Which one do you like?" Daddy asked me.

It was early evening, Daddy and I were at St. Anne's trying to select a dress for my second grade Holy Communion ceremony. Students had to go though the ceremony first before they were allowed to accept the Communion wafer at Mass. I pointed to the cheaper dress.

"Are you sure?" Daddy asked.

"Yes."

Daddy looked at the salesman, the salesman looked at me then at Daddy.

"How come you don't like this one?" Daddy pointed to the more expensive dress.

"It . . . uh . . . I don't like it."

I wanted to say that it was ugly but using my child instinct I swallowed the word. I didn't think Daddy would be too pleased if he heard me use that word. It was true though, the more expensive dress had no embroidery and no veil like the cheaper one. I felt that the veil and the embroidery added lots of beauty to the dress. I was certain which one I wanted.

"Are you sure?" Daddy asked again making sure the salesman heard him.

"Yes."

Daddy hesitated. "OK sir, we'll take this one." Daddy pointed to the cheaper dress.

The salesman looked at me with skepticism. Daddy looked ashamed. My subconscious was aware that there was something real immature going on between these two adults. I was too excited about the dress so I ignored them.

I fell in love with that dress. It looked just like a miniature white wedding dress, and boy did I fantasize. One day I got the chance to act out my fantasy.

Me and Moosey went over to the section of housing units where Sareeda lived. Sareeda and Moosey wanted to play the roles of priest so they got this wild idea to marry me off. I was more than willing to play up to my part so I snuck my communion dress out of the house. Roy was a couple of years older than I. Like most of the girls in the neighborhood, I thought he was the cutest boy around. Sareeda and Moosey dressed him in his father's four-sizes-too-big suit jacket and tie. Some of our friends gathered around us.

"Cindy, do you take Roy to be your lawfully wedded husband?"
"Yeah."
"Roy, do you do the same?"
"Uh huh."
". . . ."
"Put the rang on her finger."
Roy hesitantly slipped the band-aid on my finger.
"OK, you can kiss each other now."

I moved my head forward to kiss Roy. He drew back. He sure wasn't too enthusiastic. I think it was because I was his little brother's girlfriend. But I was sincere and I wanted a kiss. I grabbed his head and pushed his lips onto my face. Roy ran off into Sareeda's brother's room.

For the reception we served Vienna sausages and crackers for hors d'oeuvres and cherry Kool-aid for champagne; stuff that we had taken from my parents kitchen shelf. I went into an adjacent room to see what my new husband was doing. To my bewilderment, some of my girlfriends were standing in line waiting their turn to get a kiss from Roy. Boy, was I pissed! That was the end of that marriage.

******

The smell of cheap perfume and cologne filled the inside of Daddy's station wagon. Mama and Daddy sat up front while we siblings crammed into the back seats of the car. It was Sunday morning and we were on our way to mass at St. Anne's. Daddy always walked to the upper middle or front pews. I hated that, especially when we were late. Marching down the aisle in a single file line, our dark skin became brilliantly bright against the white robes the priest wore and the white parishioners. Everybody stared at us like we were exhaling a plague. It was awfully scary being in a place so sacred and holy, yet feeling so uncomfortable and insecure.

I dreaded when Mass ended for Daddy and Mama usually waited in the rear of the church to greet the priests. This was also where the confession booth was located. Every Wednesday my class had to walk over to the church, which was adjoined to the school building, to face the sins we had committed that preceding week. That booth inevitably reminded me of some of my first humiliating confessions.

When kneeling down, I always placed my fingers on the edge of the sill. This was to give myself leverage up to the window that was a little above my head. The window wasn't solid, there were tiny holes carved into the wood. I could see the light reflecting from inside the small compartment where the priest sat.

"Forgive me . . . uh . . . uh." I could never fully remember the verse that I was supposed to say before revealing my sins, so the priest always helped me. "Forgive me father, for I have sinned."

I repeated, "Forgive me father, for I have sinned."

"I haven't made a confession since last Wednesday."

"I haven't made a confession since last Wednesday," I nervously skipped back. "Forgive me father for I have sinned."

"What did you do?"

"I stole ten cents from my mother's purse."

The priest then conveyed my sin to God, asked that I be forgiven and led away from temptation. The following Wednesday came.

"Forgive me uh, uh."

"Forgive me father for I have sinned."

I repeated, "Forgive me father for I have sinned."

"I haven't made a confession since last Wednesday."

"I haven't had my last confession since last Wednesday."

"What did you do?"

"I stole twenty cents from my mother's purse."

Again the priest conveyed my sin to God and asked that I be forgiven and led a way from temptation. The next Wednesday came.

"Uh . . . uh . . . forgive."

"Forgive me father for I have si. . ." I stepped in. "For I have sinned. I haven't had, uh." He assisted again. "Made a confession since Wednesday."

"My last confession since Wednesday."

"What did you do?"

"I stole a quarter from my mother's purse."

I guess my voice and transgression had become familiar to him. This time the young and rather curious priest slid the window open and peeked out at me for a moment. He had beady eyes and dark brown, prim-cut hair. His face was expressionless. My fingers felt dirty, so I drew them back closer to the edge of the sill. The priest slid the window closed and conveyed my sin.

It was awful. Wednesday after Wednesday, before my turn came to enter the booth, I nervously sat in the pew and tried to figure out what sin I was going to confess. While I waited, I'd escape inside the stained glass windows that were high above on the walls and behind the altar. The windows were iconographed. The haloed angels and saints wore faces of calamity and radiance. The heavens were in the pastel and sometimes misty blue and grey skies. I hovered with the saints in those skies and walked on top of and through the clouds. Though visible to one another, our eyes never met and we had no voices. Their presence was as solid as my breath. Silence stood strong and thought was so free that it was obsolete. In one particular window I sat with David on the back of his horse. Strength and honor was ours for Goliath had already been defeated. Tranquility overshadowed us. I felt wonderful.

Actually the real truth is that I never had done what I said I did. Swiping money form my Mama's purse seemed to be a perfect mischievous deed so that's what I always confessed. Besides, I couldn't, because of anxiety think of anything else. I was so naive that I committed a sin so that I could be forgiven for one. There were times when I wanted to say I hadn't done anything. Though, my subconscious was aware that it I had done this, then the whole purpose behind me entering the booth would have been eluded.

There are times when I have wondered if I am partially to blame for that stereotype about black people being nothing but thieves. I wondered if that young priest had told some of his friends about my confessions. Then they in turn passed it one and soon the stereotype was developed in the grapevine. On the other hand, I have often wondered about the destiny of the priest. Considering that I kept confessing the same transgression over and over again, I wondered if that priest, my channel to God, felt a lack of credibility and kept my confessions a secret. I imagined that he quit the priesthood and became a salesman or politician.

After confession on Wednesdays we went through the regular mass format before returning to class. There was always another class, Sister Theresa's seventh grade group, that occupied the church along with my class. The seventh graders waited until we finished our confessions and then we had mass together. Sister Theresa's group always received communion first. There was this one chubby, blond-haired seventh grader that almost scared me to death. She gave me my first insight into the world of phobia.

With her hands folded together and her arms resting in her lap, she approached the kneeling bench that was before the altar. Her pale face showed no expression and she walked as if she was in a trance. Slowly she kneeled and rested her hands on top of the bannister. The priest walked along the other side of the bannister administering communion. He moved in front of her. "Body of Christ."

"Amen," her lips formed.

The priest inserted the host into her mouth.

Slump! her limp body dangled over the bannister. The priest moved along. Sister Theresa with a disappointed and upset look on her face, yanked Chubby up by her plaid uniform. She quickly came to and Sister Theresa and another student led her to the pew in the front row. The student vigorously fanned Chubby's blushed face while Sister Theresa looked on with disgust.

Time after time the same thing happened. Chubby passed out and Sister Theresa got pissed. I suddenly feared going up to receive communion. It didn't look like a pleasant situation to be in. What was it that made her do that? I constantly wondered. Maybe there was something there that made her do that, something that no one else could see but her. Supernatural thoughts swayed into my mind. I vowed to myself that I would not kneel in the same spot where Chubby always knelt. Maybe there was something there that overpowered her and took control of her.

Because of the way I was situated in the pew, a couple of times I did end up having to kneel in the same spot as Chubby. Though timid and anticipating something to happen, my knees never buckled. There were times when other students fainted but Chubby stood out because she always fainted. Wednesday after Wednesday I watched Chubby kneel down and Sister Theresa stare with anticipation.

Slump! and over the bannister she'd go.

What a geek! I thought.

Unlike St. Anne's, M.B. Baptist Church sat like a sheik's palace. The roof was shaped like a dome and there were large white pillars upholding its enormous structure. M.B. Baptist Church sat on the corner directly across the street from my housing unit. It stood overlooking the busy Walker expressway.

Late one Saturday afternoon I was feeling extremely eager to know. "Mama, can I go to M.B. with Ruby Mae?"

"Yeah, I guess so, as long as you put this in church." She handed me twenty cents. "and you don't stay all day."

Of course Mama wouldn't have okayed this if Daddy was at home. Furthermore, I wouldn't have even bothered to ask. Even with religion Daddy wanted his family to be different. Mama wasn't so choosy. Regardless of what church I attended, if I gave an offering and prayed, Mama felt satisfied.

"You hafta sit in da back for a little while by yo'self, cuz I hafta sit in da front and watch my granmama git baptize," Ruby Mae explained.

"Are there going to be a lot of people there?" I asked.

"I don't know, maybe, maybe not."

"What's the holy ghost?" I had heard my friends sporadically talking about getting the holy ghost so I wasn't sure exactly what it was.

"You don't know what dat is?" Her expression told me to give her a break. "Dat be when da spirit comes into yo' body and you start jumpin' up and down and talkin' in different tongue."

"What's tongue?"

"You know, different words and stuff."

"Is it a bad spirit?"

"Nope, it makes you happy. When you be jumpin' up and down dat jus means you be very happy. But you cain't control yo'self cuz da spirit is too strong."

"Oh."

"You hafta watch out too, cuz those big ladies will knock you down if you be in da way when dey git the spirit."

We giggled. We ran across the street swinging our patent leather black purses.

"Hi Lucas!"

"Hi Lucas."

Old man Lucas never said too much. Always concentrating on his newspapers, he stayed too busy for chitchat. His barely sustaining newspaper stand was on the side of the church. The thin wood, of almost cardboard-like material, hung off to the sides of its weak and limp foundation. The newspaper stand looked certain to fall if a small wind came by.

Lucas moved as if he had a slight case of cerebral palsy. His head, arms and legs constantly twitched and jerked. When he made his rounds through the neighborhood, the metallic shopping cart that he pushed, which had loose and wobbly wheels, moved in unison with his body. Whenever Lucas pushed that cart over a bump in the sidewalk or street, the quaking earth that seemed to follow underneath him soared. That squeaky cart got louder and they both shook uncontrollably.

"Hey Too-Too."

"Hey y'all." Too-Too worked with Lucas on the weekends and sometimes after school. He sometimes complained about how long their delivery rounds would take because of how slow Lucas walked. But overall, he seemed to enjoy helping the old man out. Besides, the small pocket change he received was a plus.

"Where y'all going?" Too-Too asked.

"To church. Ruby Mae's granmama is getting baptized."

"Better not buy no candy with that money Mom gave you, better put it in church. I know she gave you some."

"So!" I said.

"Better watch out for that holy ghost too," he said teasingly.

"Forgit you boy," I said.

I could not believe the immense space inside M.B. The pews seemed endless and the dome-shaped ceiling seemed as far away as the sky. From the rear pews, the high platform in front of the church looked miniature.

"Come on, you can sit close to da front cuz it's not crowded today."

"Wait, hold my hand," I said.

Ruby Mae led me to an empty pew that was behind and off to the side of the pews in the front, which were filled. Ruby Mae periodically glimpsed back at me and waved.

The giant-sized aquarium that sat up on the platform totally confused me. The tank was filled with water that was light green in color and non-transparent. I was used to seeing the priest hold the person's head over a ceramic bowl or dish and let water trickle on the person's forehead; seemingly simple and uncomplicated. What in the heck were they doing with a big fish tank on the stage? I asked myself.

Three people entered onto the platform. Their bodies were wrapped in white garments and the tops of their heads were also wrapped in a white garment. From where I was sitting, I couldn't pinpoint which one was Ruby Mae's grandmother. Actually, I couldn't distinguish if the three were all women, two women and one man, or one woman and two men. They all appeared upper aged because of their frail-looking bodies and they were all pretty much the same height. The white garments made them look like identical triplets.

The pastor stepped down into the tank first. Then, what (I assumed to be a woman) approached the tank. Her fragile and tiny body started trembling wildly. There was this loud, vibrating, moaning sound and I could hear her teeth clicking together. I had never seen anything quite like this. I imagined her as a wind up toy, someone had wound her up and forgot to turn her off. "Hee hee hee hee hee ha ha hee." I tried to but I couldn't stop. I giggled and I laughed and I giggled. I leaned forward holding my tickled stomach. The tickles were so intense that my stomach hurt. I looked around and to my surprise, no one else was laughing. Everybody stared at the tank as if they had been hypnotized. No one even seemed to notice that I was laughing. I tried real hard to hold back my giggles. I couldn't believe how difficult it was for me to stop myself from laughing. Every time I thought about that stupid wind up toy, I had periodic outbursts.

Finally, the trembling woman stood in the water. The reverend held on to her. *Dunk*! Oh my God! I don't believe it, he dunked her in. He really dunked her in. When he lifted her out of the water she smoothly released her breath. My giggling stopped. She wasn't trembling anymore. Her arms bounced up and down. When they went up her fingers were grasping, as though she was trying to touch something. The woman let out a joyous yell, "Halle-luu-jah!" A gentleman came and helped her out of the tank. He helped her dry off. Her frail body didn't appear so frail anymore. I felt a cool breeze all over my body. It was incredible. I felt so refreshed. This totally blew me away; I had never quite experienced anything like it. I watched closely as the others were baptized. I, too, became mesmerized.

For the life of me, I couldn't understand why that lady was so afraid before she had entered the tank. It was the first time that I had ever seen someone so full of fear. I had to give myself an answer. In my mind, I myself was standing over the giant sized tank.

The water is so dense, I can't see through it. I don't want to put my feet in—there could be something in there. Yep, I am sure. There is something in there and it is waiting for me. What, I don't know but there is something. That's it. I have found out what frightened that lady. It's that thick green water. The water blocked her vision. She couldn't see what was waiting for her, but she knew that it was something magnificent; cuz she could feel it, all through her body. I felt scared just like that lady but I wasn't trembling, was not aware enough about this magnificence to tremble—did not feel it.

Even on Sundays, when Daddy wasn't home, if Mama didn't feel like walking to St. Anne's she would permit me and my sisters and brothers to go to M.B. with our friends, if we wanted. Before church me and my friends always went to the candy store. We stuffed our small patent leather purses with candy and chewing gum until we couldn't close the zippers. Sometimes I used half the money Mama gave me to put into church.

Up and down the stairs and long halls we ran. Next to a flight of stairs that led up to the balcony hung a picture of civil rights leader, Dr. Martin Luther King. I always stopped to look at it. His dreamy eyes were like glass, I could see right through them. Anything that I wanted to imagine, I could see in those dark piercing eyes. It was definitely a picture most people stopped to stare at. Us younger kids hardly ever sat through the whole church service. The times when we'd sit in, I always anticipated someone getting the holy ghost. Unlike at St. Anne's, if someone felt something powerful at M.B., they sure didn't hold back. This was fine with me, in fact I found it quite exhilarating. I also liked the solitude at St. Anne's but I hated the uncomfortableness.

At M.B. I sat in on a couple of Bible study classes with some other kids. The classes were held in a small room in the basement of the church. In the corner of the room sat a few wooden instruments. A wood piano was in the front of the room. The instruments were kept immaculately clean and they shone brightly. The room carried a strong smell of wood. I can remember trying to understand what they were discussing but it all seemed way over my head. Everything that I was trying to comprehend was all wrapped up in the smell of that wood. I would later make that smell a reminder of my days there at M.B.

Chapter 10

I had managed to get myself inside the park. The baseball game was just beginning and people were rushing in, trying to get to their seats. I must have been looking towards the ground because when I looked up, there she was. I didn't see her approaching and I don't think that she saw me approaching, our eyes simply happened to meet. Her eyes grew a bit wide. "Hi Cindy!" Her smile slowly went away as she noticed my mismatched clothes, torn shoes and oversized pants. My lips partially spread. She continued hesitantly. "This is my little brother, Jeremy." Jeremy spontaneously smiled at me and I smiled back. How cute he was, I thought. Just like his sister he had curly red hair and a face full of freckles. He wore new looking clothes and a jolly smile to go along with them—perfect just like they should be, I pondered. Tracy pointed at me. "Look Dad, that's the girl in my class at school." Dad was an exact copy of Jeremy only Dad stood like a tower. Jeremy and Tracy looked awfully tiny standing next to Dad. Dad looked over at me. "What a cute little monkey," he said. I suppose he thought that I was going to chuckle too. He stooped a bit, put his arms around Tracy and Jeremy and quickly led them away. They turned to look at me as Dad nudged them into the other direction. I felt a heavy pressure in my chest as though someone was pressing down on it. I could feel the temperature rising in my face—I felt really warm. My eyes and my head lowered. I had the immense need to be with someone so that everybody would know that I wasn't a stray. I ran home and got my six-year-old brother to come back up to the ball park with me. I wished that Daddy could come and the rest of my family too. That was like thinking the impossible. Daddy stayed on the road most of the time, and even if not, the tickets to the games were too expensive for the whole family to attend. Nevertheless, having my little brother with me was better than having no one at all, I thought.

It was around the fourth inning when we ran into Broomhead. "Hey Broomhead, can you give us some money?" I asked. "We wanna git us something to eat."

"Go over to Jon's hot dog stand," he pointed. "There's a fat girl over there wearing a pony tail. She's in one of my classes at school, just tell her who you are and she'll give you some free food."

"Ok."

"Does Mama know ya'll up here?"

"Yes." I was lying.

"After ya'll get something to eat, go home! You don't need to be running around up here—it's dangerous."

Me and my little brother ran off to the hot dog stand. I raised my hand above the counter. I didn't see anyone. I heard some water running in the back so we waited in front of the large window. Finally from around the corner came none other than the fainting queen herself. It was Chubby. Now I understood why she was so plump. Chubby looked at me as though my face was familiar to her. "Whata you guys have?" She asked me so quickly that I hadn't gotten the chance to tell her that I was Louis' little sister. I felt hurried so I started ordering. "I want a cheeseburger a order of fries and a chocolate shake." I turned to my little brother. "What do you want?"

"Get me some french fries and a coke and some hot dog and a candy bar."

Chubby heard him so I didn't have to relay his order. While she prepared our food I prayed hard that she knew who I was because we didn't have money to pay for all that stuff.

"Here you go." She smiled and put the food on top of the counter. "Tell Louis I said hello." I felt so relieved. Chubby isn't such a geek after all, I thought. Me and my little brother went around to the side of the hot dog stand. We sat on the edge of the sidewalk and ate our food. Some white people that walked by or drove their cars past us stared at us with disgust.

Later that evening Sistine had been occupying the bathroom for at least fifteen minutes. To me it seemed like two hours. "Maaama, Sistine's been in the bathroom for too long and I hav'ta get in."

"Sistine, hurry up and come outta there and let your sister git in."

"Dag, cain't even use the toilet in peace," Sistine said as she exited.

The ivory suds trickled down my arms. There was not a speck of dirt to be seen mixed within the suds. I stuck my hands and arms down into the running water. The ivory suds moved down the drain. My black left hand grabbed onto the hot water nozzle, I turned it up a bit more. I was helping Mom do the laundry one day and she told me that hot water sterilized things, cleaned off germs better. The bar of soap vigorously slipped and slid through my hands, I wanted to get all the lather possible. Darn! I thought, the lather was still pure ivory. The suds moved down the drain. Vigorously the bar of soap slipped and slid in my hands again. There was a slight burning sensation on the backs of my hands now. It wasn't painful enough though to keep me from scrubbing. I held my black hands up to the light. It was unbelievable, I didn't understand; the dirt couldn't come off. That darkness, that blackness was me. I stood behind my eyes and looked out at those hands. I wanted to walk off and leave them in suspension but my body stood in the way.

******

Women, ladies and girls came together in crowds. It was ladies' day at the ball park; all females entered the park free of admission. The ushers readied themselves for a possible full house. They stood guarding the gates in their tidy white hats and gloves and their dark blue suits with fine yellow trimming; looking all too patriotic. The game had entered into the third inning. People were still coming in but the entrance gates weren't nearly as crowded as they were before the game had started. A young girl walked up to the entrance gate. There were about eight ushers standing about two feet away from one another. The girl switched her hips from side to side as she approached one of the ushers. "Excuse me, sir," she said in an extremely high voice. "Is it ladies' day?" Her skirt fit tightly around her full waist. A scarf covered most of her hair, except for her bangs that lay nicely on her forehead. One large pink barrette was snapped onto the center of her bangs. She flicked her eyelashes up and down at the usher. How cute she is, the usher thought. What a little darling. "Of course it is, you just come right on in. Are you going to watch the game all by yourself?"

"Well, my friends are supposed to meet me up here," she said in her high voice, grinning and blushing at the usher.

The young usher stepped aside and the girl passed through the gate. He watched her swaying hips as she walked off onto one of the ramps. The other ushers snickered at him.

The girl walked up the ramp and over to one of the railings on the side of the ramp. She peeked her head from behind a large iron pillar and looked down. All the ushers were in clear view. She quickly removed her skirt revealing a pair of beige shorts that she wore underneath. She held the skirt in her hand and leaned over the railing. She yelled down at the ushers in a lower voice. "Nah-nah-nah-nah nah." The ushers looked up. Broomhead snatched the scarf and barrette from his hair and put them in his hand with the skirt. He dangled and waved the garments over the rail. Broomhead yelled down at them laughing uncontrollably. "A-ha, nah-nah-nah-nah nah. Suckers, suckers. I got you this time." The usher that allowed Broomhead to pass put his hand on top of his head. "Oh my God!" The ushers broke into laughter. The suckered usher took off running up the ramp after Broomhead. Broomhead took off running with the garments swinging in his hand. It was no use, Broomhead knew Lions Park like the back of his hand. There was no way that usher was going to catch him.

Chapter 11

"Come on git up, it's time ta go ta school" Mama moved her short, thin body from room to room. I slept on the side of the bed that was pushed up against the wall. The best part about waking up in the morning was when I crawled over Pepe in order to get out of bed. Of course I could have easily crawled down to the bottom of the bed but there was something stirring about crawling over her massive body. As I went over I would apply all of my weight on her. Pepe, being a heavy sleeper, never woke up, but it was fun watching her twitch. I sat on the edge of the bed with my upper body curled over and my elbows resting on my knees. I knew I had no choice but to get going, though I wasn't too sure if I wanted to or not. Things that happened to us while traveling back and forth to St. Anne's were pretty unpredictable. Would we be chased home today? Would someone point out my blackness as if I didn't know I was black. Would someone discover the small rip in my black loafers and make fun? I never knew what to expect.

It would be perfect right now if one of us came down with an outbreak. One day Louis got the chicken pox. I eased my way into his bed and rolled around in his covers for a while. Then in just a short time, as I had planned, the mass of pimples erupted all over my body like sesame seeds on a bun. Mama came in and took one look, "Oh brother, looks like you got it too. No St. Anne's today!" It was great. Sistine came and took her turn squirming around in our covers, then David followed. One by one Mama marched us down into the kitchen and rubbed us all over with corn meal. "Ahhhh, that felt soooo good." The fiery itch in those bumps seemed to die out. I didn't have to scratch anymore like a dog going at a flea inside his collar. It would take a miracle though for my chicken pox scheme to happen again, for our systems were already immune to that army of pimples. It had already worked twice.

We fought our way in and out of the bathroom.

"Hurry up boy, we ain't got all day."

"Git out of da way, girls go first."

"Oooooh I'm telling Mama. Maamaa! David sittin on the toilet sleepin."

Mama made oatmeal again for breakfast. I hated oatmeal. I poured milk on mine to take away the slimy feeling when the oatmeal went down my throat. I ate my whole bowlful because I was hungry. Louis dumped mounds of sugar on his as if he were going to eat it, then slid his bowl onto the edge of the table, hoping that it would fall off. What a cop out! Like me, Sistine and David had bellies that wanted to be filled, so they gulped down their oatmeal. Louis shrieked as he imagined the large clumps of oatmeal riding down our throats.

Daddy came downstairs. I was surprised, I didn't know that he had come home. Must have had a short trip. Daddy pulled out a plate of sandwiches from the refrigerator. Three were wrapped in aluminum foil and two in wax paper. There were four brown lunch bags lined up on the counter next to the kitchen sink. Daddy set the plate of sandwiches next to the bags. "Y'all can put your own sandwiches in your own lunch bags. I have ta git outta here, the train pulls out at eight o'clock." What! Daddy was letting us pack our own lunch? Louis, sitting with his side facing the counter, spotted the aluminum foil wrapping by looking from the corner of his eye. He didn't turn his head for he didn't dare to be so obvious with Daddy in our presence. Sistine was sitting facing the counter so she couldn't help but keep her eyes glued to the plate. We all started up our motors. Our motors were on idle for we weren't about to leap with Daddy still standing in the kitchen. "Don't be acting like no wild animals like you ain't never had nothing before!" he'd probably yell. Then he would surely take a forceful yank at our noses, and no one wanted to be subjected to that.

Daddy started in the direction toward the steps, and we all slid onto the edge of our seats. Cheating David was half standing up and half sitting down. "Brrrm, brrrm, brrrrm." We waited until Daddy got halfway up the stairs.

Zoom!

Zoom. The race was on.

"Woah," Sistine almost got me in the face with her fat elbow. "Shoot!" I almost had that one before David's arm reached in. Un un no way. I don't want to be stuck with a wax paper sandwich. "Aww, aww, that's no fair. I didn't get one," I whimpered. "Come on David, change wit me."

"Un un," he clung on to his aluminum foil-wrapped sandwich.

My whimpering got louder. "Aw, aw, but I don't want this." I picked at the wax paper. I felt so unfortunate, I started to blubber loudly.

"What da hell is going on down there?" Daddy came running down the stairs. His checkered black and white work pants were unzipped. There I was, standing with my eyes full of tears. "They took all the sandwiches in aluminum foil."

"How come you don't want dese ones in the wax paper?" He pointed to the two remaining sandwiches that were left on the plate.

"Cuz, they suck!" Nope, I didn't say it. That phrase was buried somewhere underneath the thickness inside my complex brain. Besides, amongst other reasons I valued my teeth. "Because, I don't know why," I answered. Daddy snatched up the plate and flung the sandwiches back into the refrigerator. "Well den, eat some damn air pies!"

There it was, that feeling. That is the main reason why I couldn't tell him that his sandwiches sucked. I am certain that I would have gotten a lash for saying that word. But I believe there also would have been lashes stemming from that feeling that he would have absorbed, when I informed him of my dislike for his expression of tender loving care. Ok Daddy, if that's the way it had to be, "eat some damn air pies." Boy that really sunk my emotions. Louis, David, and Sistine thought it was all pretty funny. They hid behind Daddy snickering and chuckling at me.

I turned down Tommy's half of sandwich. And someone, someone just had to say something. "Dumb poor blackie." It was that kid that sat behind me. He had a nose like Pinochio and deep blond hair. He always looked at me like he wanted to throw a loop around my neck any second. Though I heard him loud and clear, I pretended that I didn't. I wasn't going to dare turn around and look at him; there was no way that I wanted to risk getting a noose around my neck.

On the way home Sareeda started it up again. "Hey Cindy, you catch any air pies today? Hee hee hee."

"A ha ha ha."

"Bet dem air pies taste pretty good, don't they? Hee hee hee." Sistine joked.

David had to get in on the fun, too. "Hey Cindy, can yo spell air pies? Ay eye r pea eye eeeeee s."

I giggled. This was great. That which had been terribly emotional for me, was now quite humorous. I was glad now that they found it so funny. Life was worth the struggle with people like them around.

******

We had walked halfway through the viaduct. Me, Sistine and Sareeda gossiped while the boys led the way to school in front of us.

"I think another black family may be coming to school with us," Sareeda mentioned.

"How you know?"

"I saw them in the office yesterday."

"Is it a big family?" I inquired.

"All I saw was a girl and two boys."

"I sure hope so, it's about time we got some."

Sareeda interrupted Sistine. "Hey Sistine, are we going to get her today?"

"Shhh, don't say nothing about that. I don't want her to know." Sistine looked over at me.

"Know what?" I asked.

"Nothin!" Sistine replied.

"Come on, I won't tell, I promise. Sareeda tell me."

"They both ignored my pleading. We came from out of the viaduct, walking a couple of feet behind the boys now. David whispered. "Uh oh, here comes a Dick." There was a dark blue car approaching, heading in the opposite direction.

"What's a Dick?" I questioned David.

"That's what we call an unmarked police car. Those be cops in that car."

The car slowed down as it got closer to us. The two white officers that were wearing dark suits and ties, became visible. I threw up my hand to wave. The man in the passenger seat tapped the driver on the shoulder if to say, watch this. The officer leaned towards the front window. He put his hand on the dashboard. As the car slowly passed by us he flipped us his middle finger. My hand quickly sank.

"Did you see that? They gave us the finger." Ricky was just as surprised as I was.

Our pace quickened. How could they feel that way about us? I thought they were all Officer Friendlies, I meditated. I am certainly going to stop in the warehouse after school today.

I trampled alone over the cans of paint and wood beams. I worked my way around the stacked boxes and tall shelves. I knew that I would find him soon. I peeked around a corner and there he was, the robust white man.

"Hi" I said.

He looked up at me. "Hi."

"Bye," I said.

"Bye," he said.

I trampled my way out and caught up with the rest.

Sistine and Sareeda had taken my momentary absence for granted.

"How come you didn't hit her?"

"By the time I got over there it was too many people standing around."

"When I first signaled you should have come, there wasn't hardly anybody over there."

"We have to get her tomorrow cuz I'm sick of her calling me monkey girl all the time. I'm going to teach her a lesson." Sistine was determined.

"Who?" I asked. They ignored me. "Y'all might as well tell because I already heard y'all talking about beating somebody up."

"Cindy if you tell Dad I'm going to kill you, I swear it. And I ain't gonna ever let you use my brand new pencil case again neither."

Wow, what a threat. That pencil case you're talking about is two years old, and you're still calling it brand new. "Tell what? I'm not goin' to tell."

"Me and Sareeda are going to get this girl at school for calling me names."

"Oh."

When we arrived home there was a chocolate doughnut on the kitchen table and I grabbed for it.

"Oooooh, give me some," Sistine whined.

"No! I got it first."

"Better share!"

"I'm not gonna share anything, I got it first."

"Give me some," Sistine yelled as she snatched at the doughnut.

"Keep it up and I'm gonna tell Daddy you beat up that white girl at school."

Daddy was out of view behind some drawn curtains in the pantry. He bolted out of the pantry in two seconds flat. "Did what? Godamnit!"

"Beat up a girl at school."

"She's lying I didn't even touch that girl."

He grabbed Sistine by her shoulders and shook her violently. "Damn you! Damn you! Don't you ever, ever let me hear you do somethin like that again." Daddy was like a madman, he was infuriated. I didn't understand the intensity of his anger. I started feeling real guilty and sorry for telling on her.

Daddy went back into the pantry. Sistine whimpered and rolled her eyes at me. "I hate your guts! I swear as long as I live I ain't gonna never, ever share another secret with you ever!" Then I was glad again that I had told on her.

******

I received another invitation to a birthday party from a kid in my class. The Saturday of the party Daddy and I jumped in the car and headed off to Rodepoint.

"You don't remember the address at all?" Daddy asked.

"No."

"Where could you have put that invitation?"

"I don't know; I must have laid it down somewhere."

As we drove through the viaduct I was real glad that I had thrown the invitation in the trash.

"Do you have any idea what the girl's parents' car looks like?"

"I think it's a station wagon." I was being honest.

"We're going to drive around. If you see it let me know."

We drove up and down the neighborhood streets in Rodepoint, looking at cars and looking for kids wearing party hats. I began to feel guilty and I hoped that we would find the house. We didn't.

The following Monday at school one of my classmates who had attended the party walked over to me. "How come you didn't come to the party?" she asked.

"I was going to come but I lost the invitation and me and my Dad couldn't find the house."

"We were all glad you didn't come anyway. You know what we did?"

"What?"

"Every time a car pulled up we all hid behind the furniture just in case it was you. When it was someone else we came out from behind the furniture."

I shrugged my shoulders and she walked away. My eyes and my head lowered.

Chapter 12

It was seat-cushion day at the ballpark. Me and Franco were wandering inside the park. Since we hadn't paid to be admitted in the park, we didn't receive any hometown emblematized seat cushions. The game was in the fifth inning. Most people stayed in the seat stands while some moved back and forth to the bathrooms and food windows. We were up on the second level. There were a couple of bathrooms located on the second level but most of them, as well as the food stands, were down on the first level. We were up on the second level. We wandered into a remote area. There were a lot of painted steel beams and iron pipes embedded underneath the seating stands. The concrete passage that we walked on was vacant. The small ramps that led to the seats were also vacant. No one was exiting or entering the ladies room that was off into a corner. Two white boys about the same age as me and Franco, seven or eight, appeared on the passage. They were approaching us, walking in the opposite direction. "Wanna get their cushions?" I asked. Franco's eyes opened wide and then he nodded. I gave instructions. "You get one and I'll take the other one." I looked around. Except for us and the two boys, the area was still vacant. "Ok, here they come. I'm gonna git the one in the red shirt," I said.

He never saw the situation coming. I cornered the boy in the red shirt. "Give me it!" I snatched the red and white cushion out of his loosely gripping hand. *Wham*! I landed a blow to his face. He just stood there; he didn't even wince. "Wack!" I hit him in the face again. He showed no facial expressions but his skin turned blood red. Why isn't he crying? The little bastard won't cry. I got angry and felt frustrated. I looked around to see if anyone was coming, *Pow*! This time he turned his head to the side. He still didn't cry. *Knock*! I landed a blow behind his ear, right on a bone. The knock seemed to echo, his head seemed hollow to me. Jesus! What the heck is wrong with his head, feels like a rock. He doesn't even feel my punches! Maybe those white people don't have anything in their heads, I thought.

Here, one for the road. *Smack*! I slapped him on the top of his head. Finally the tears came. The boy looked at me—there was no hatred in his eyes. "Get outta here," I released him.

The two boys ran off. I felt real awkward standing there with that seat cushion. I also felt scared. What if they go back and get somebody. Franco bit down on his nails, we both knew that we had done something wrong. I grabbed the cushion from his hand and ran into the ladies' restroom. I dumped both cushions in the trash.

While we were waiting in one of the large parking lots for exiting spectators, I kept thinking about what me and Franco had done. I felt sorry about that moment. I kept seeing that red shirt and those innocent eyes. I was sorry that I had hit him like that. Everything had happened so fast. I couldn't stop thinking about those seat cushions laying in the trash. Why had I panicked like an idiot and thrown them away? What was the meaning? I didn't know. That whole moment seemed pointless.

The game went into the eighth inning. Franco and I split up; he walked out of view way over to the other side of the parking lot. I was a bit curious as to why the bigger kids hadn't come to run us out of the big lot yet. Except for Franco and me, the lot was rather isolated. This was odd considering that the game was in the eighth inning. Broomhead came from behind one of the cars in the lot. "Cindy be careful, there's Dicks around here picking up window wipers."

"Should I leave?"

"No, but if you see a white man in a dark suit comin' to you, run." Broomhead walked off.

I looked around the lot. I was feeling timid because I didn't see any other window wipers. I didn't see any Dicks neither, so I went over to wipe my first car for the day. The father slid underneath the wheel from the passenger side of the car. The kids that looked a couple of years older than I gathered into the back seat. I moved my rag across the front window on the driver's side. Without looking up at me, the father put his key in the ignition. I wiped again, still the father did not acknowledge my presence. I didn't think he understood so I stuck my hand out. The father turned towards the rear of the car and said something to the kids. I couldn't hear what he had said because the windows were rolled up. Though, I figured that he had told them to stop staring at me because they all hesitantly turned their eyes away from me. When he whipped out of the parking space, the kids couldn't keep themselves from peeking back at me. That is it—I have had enough. I hated the way that man had ignored me. He seemed like he hadn't even cared if I was standing in the path of the car wheels. I hated the way those kids looked down at me. I had had enough humiliation. At that moment I decided that I didn't want to wipe windows anymore. I had had enough. Besides, the older kids, the boys, always made the real money anyway, the big money, the dollar bills. I always ended up with a small amount of spare change. I didn't want to wipe windows anymore.

The parking lot still seemed isolated. The spectators were taking their time returning to their cars. I assumed that the game had gone into extra innings which it had. I still didn't spot anymore window wipers. Broomhead came running up to me. "This place is crawling with Dicks. Come on, I gotta figure out a way ta get us outta here, drop down that rag." I threw my rag on the ground. "Wait here, I'll be right back." Broomhead trotted off.

Way on the other side of the lot I saw four Dicks walking between the parked cars. Broomhead quickly returned from around the corner. Broomhead's right arm hung around the shoulders of a little boy. He held the boy close to his side. Although I didn't know the wiper personally, I had seen him up at the ball park many times before. Broomhead held a stick of pink cotton candy in his left hand. The cotton candy was big, fluffy and nicely formed, it was easy to see that the cotton candy had not been touched. I held the candy momentarily while my brother brushed the dust from my pants. Then he put his left arm around my shoulders and pulled me close to his side. We walked towards the main gate of the parking lot. "Don't ya'll say anything, just let me do the talkin'."

As we got closer to the gate I could now see six or seven more Dicks standing by the gate. They all wore dark blue suits and ties. Out of the corner of my eye I could also see the cotton candy that my brother held in his left hand; I didn't yet quite understand. We approached the gate, Broomhead held us tightly to his side. One of the Dicks walked toward us. "None of you guys wouldn't happen to be any of those window washers would ya?"

"No sir. I just came from taking my little brother and sister to the baseball game." Broomhead tilted the cotton candy forward a bit. The little boy looked so unlike me and Broomhead that it was hysterical.

"Where you headin'?" The astute preppy-looking Dick wasn't giving in too quickly. His eyes searched all three of us from head to toe.

"We're on our way home sir, just came to enjoy the game, now we're heading home sir."

The Dick stared at us. I felt that he really knew we were window wipers. I imagined that there was a tiny voice inside of his head. "Com'on, let 'em go. Come on, they're just a bunch of kids. Won't do no harm just to let 'em go. Besides, they have a good excuse and you didn't catch them in the ol' act. Whata you say? Just let 'em go, huh?"

The Dick succumbed. "Ok." He stepped aside. It was difficult for him to take his eyes off of Broomhead. For a fraction of a minute, I believe that white man admired the juvenile black boy who was giving him a snow job.

"All riiight, all riiight!" Broomhead said triumphantly underneath his breath.

When we got on the other side of the gate, sitting next to the curb was a dark blue Ford L.T.D. It was loaded with our window wiper friends. They looked out at us with their sullen faces. I didn't think that anyone would squeal on us but the thought did enter my mind. I thought it rather humorous that they had been caught and we hadn't. "Don't laugh, that ain't funny," Broomhead whispered. Their sullen faces stuck in my mind.

They were released around dinner time that evening. I ran up to Freddy. "What happens to you when they take you to the police station?"

"Oh, they jus take yo' money and call yo' mama. Should see all da money dey have up on da table. Dey tell you if dey catch you again you gon go ta jail."

"They don't let you keep a little bit of your money?"

"Nope, dey took everythang I made."

All I could see was this long table loaded with all the window wipers' money and white men standing over it. This made me upset. I didn't understand why they took their money; the wipers hadn't stolen it.

Of course the window wiping continued but for me it was no longer an addiction. I periodically wiped at the park but overall window wiping had become too frustrating. I submitted to playing more jump rope and hop-scotch.

******

I made a mad dash back to the school sidewalk.

"Sister Mary, Sister, Sister, can you help? Can you call the police? David's having a fight."

The habit-dressed nun looked over at the group of kids that had crowded in front of Fabia's store. "There's nothing I can do about it. It's off school grounds." She sounded very nonchalant.

At that moment I had a flashback of the white boy that I had punched at the ballpark. I thought about how he had not cried. No matter how many times I had punched him, until the final smack, he hadn't cried. I felt strong. I knew that nun didn't care one way or the other. I wasn't going to let her hurt me with her coldness. I shrugged my shoulders. By the time I got back to Fabia's, the crowd was gone and the fight had never taken place. "What happened?"

Ricky explained, "Nothing. David said, 'Hit me.' Then he said, 'No you hit me first.' Then David said, 'You take first lick.' Then they just walked off from each other cuz nobody wanted to take the first lick."

"Know what? I asked the Sister to get the police and she said," I exaggerated by sticking my nose in the air, "It's off school grounds; there ain't nothing I can do about it."

"They always say that crap. If she wanted to do something she could. It doesn't make a difference," Sistine explained.

I knew that my judgment about the nun had been correct.

******

My little brother, Ralph, entered the second grade at St. Anne's. I moved on up to the third grade and Louis went on to high school. Daddy appointed David as the new man in charge of delivering the tuition payments, which were always late, and keeping his siblings in line.

The first, second and third graders were going to have a party. All kids were told to bring a bag of candy or some kind of treat to share. I desperately explained to Mama that one bag of candy would not be enough because me and Ralph were in separate classes. Mama couldn't be convinced. On the way to school I selfishly persuaded my little brother to give me the whole bag of candy. I figured the situation wouldn't be as embarrassing for him if he just said he had nothing, rather than trying to disperse a few pieces of candy to twenty-five of his classmates. Besides, I told myself that the other kids would share with him regardless. I myself anticipated humiliation if I didn't fulfill my end of the bargain, so I took the whole bag.

I happily passed out my treats. I received lots of goodies in return. To my surprise a couple of my classmates didn't bring anything. It was no big deal; everyone shared with them anyway, including me. Our party had just gotten on its way when Ralph's teacher came over to my classroom. My teacher, Miss Mary Pat, exited the room with her. When my teacher returned she asked me to step out in the hall with her. Looking down at me she scorned, "Why does your brother not have any candy? He's sitting over there and he doesn't have anything. Why didn't he bring some treats?" She looked at me hard and paused for a response. Blood rushed to my face, I shrunk to half my size. She led me over to my brother's classroom. "Look at him! He doesn't have anything."

While the other kids were playing, my brother sat at his empty-top desk with his hands folded. I couldn't believe it, no one had shared any of their treats with him.

"Would you like to share some of your treats with your brother?" his teacher asked. She softly directed her light blue eyes at me, as if she was blind to the fact that she had initiated this whole embarrassing scene.

"Yes."

Along with Miss Mary Pat I went back to my room. I got some of my candy and took it over to my brother. I spent the rest of the day feeling alienated and exposed. Why had things gotten to the point that they had? I remembered that some of my classmates had come empty-handed. No one had seemed to make an issue about that. I sensed that my brother and I had been singled out. I also felt that I had been in a no-win situation. There is no good reason for me being over here, I thought, in a totally different place that has no space for me other than to humiliate and make fun of my existence.

After that incident I really knew that I didn't want to go to school at St. Anne's. I wished that I was back at Dalbot. I would rather put up with those harsh-sounding bells—there was no doubt in my mind.

Chapter 13

It was summer 1973. Daddy laid his huge, brown workbag on the kitchen table. Two hams, a roast, a few pounds of butter, aluminum foil and saran wrap were removed and put into our freezer. "Here you go, take this." He handed me a large box of candy that was so recognizable to me. The box had its familiar stripes around its border. The name Pan Am Rail was spelled out in big bold white letters on the front panel of the box.

I took the box outside where my friend's fingers searched inside the box. Ruby Mae held onto the empty box. "Where ya'll be gittin all dis candy from?" she asked.

"My Daddy makes a lot of money at his job. He buys it from the store."

"Oh. Can I keep dis box?"

"Un un." I took the box back.

******

For us project kids, summertime always seemed to be full of the same activities year after year. There were no trips to Disneyland or for that matter, no trips beyond our state border. Daddy found the train too abrasive for little girls but once in a blue moon my brothers got the opportunity to go away with Daddy on his job. This enabled them to travel to other states. However, those opportunities were rare, so we all just got involved in whatever was happening in the neighborhood. Of course, there was lots of money to be made at the ball park. When the Chicago Lions were away from home the boys did what they could to keep themselves entertained.

I pushed my way through their door. Tiny intricate and large pieces of plastic were strewn about on their beds.

"Get outta here!"

"Hey, which one are you guys gonna do today?" I asked.

"I don't know. Wait til we finish, den you'll see. *Slam!*" Their bedroom door shut behind them.

As usual, I sat at the top of our thirteen-step, bare-floored staircase that was next to their bedroom. I waited for five or ten minutes, then I knocked at their door. *Rap rap rap rap.*

"Go away, we're not done yet." Too-Too and Broomhead yelled.

I sat on the top step again. After fifteen minutes of anticipation I commenced to knocking at their door again. *Rap rap rap, rap rap rap, rap rap.*

"Go away, you're messin' with our concentration."

"Can I come in?"

"No! Girls don't do this kinda stuff, they're not smart enough." Too-Too said.

Guess girls are only supposed ta learn ta say big words and stuff. Not build and make things and figure things out, I thought.

I went and got a drink of water and watched a little bit of television. Then I sat on the stoop again for a few minutes, just to be safe, then I went back. *Boom! boom! boom! boom!* No answer. I removed the loose knob from their door and took a peek inside. Still hunched over their beds. Back to the step.

Finally their door opened.

"Check this baby out."

"Yeah, check mine out too."

"Oooooh oooh." I stood there oooohing away while I admired their plastic modeled Thunderbirds, antique Fords, Corvettes and sometimes yachts. Their models were always so detailed. Headlights, white wall tires and handles for every door. The exterior of the models shined immaculately, perfect for a collector's display or a showroom. I was fascinated by how they could take what seemed to be nothing, bits and pieces of plastic, and create something so fine.

While my brothers had raced to get their models completed, their buddies were at home doing the same thing. After the first person finished he would pick out someone's porch and the rest would gather accordingly, after finishing their models.

"That is toooo bad."

"Man, check out da wheels on dis baby."

"Dude dat is down, all da way live."

"Larry's is better dan that."

"Un un, his got glue oozing out from da sides."

They'd go on until finally deciding on the best model. Some of us girls would gather around them and give our ooohs and ahhhs. The louder our ooohs and ahhhs over a certain model, the more leverage to the possible winner. The winner was usually determined by how many flaws his model had and by the amount of time that was taken in order to complete the model. To me they were all perfect and I just couldn't understand why there had to be a best. Though, like the other girls, I never commented much. I only gave my ooohs and ahhhs, for my understanding was that constructing models was strictly a boys' thing. If there was one thing that the boys got into and didn't want the girls involved in, it was when they were constructing their plastic models. Secluding themselves in their bedroom was an ultimate high for them and they definitely didn't want any "silly" girls hanging around. Deep down inside I wanted to be able to take my hands and make it all happen just the way they did. Though, I never bothered to ask if I could participate, for just as I said before, I understood that this was strictly a "boys' thing."

There were rare moments when Too-Too pretended he really considered what I thought about his model. "Does that little bit of glue really look bad on my bumper?"

"Not really."

"Hey Cindy, tell the truth, isn't mine really better than all theirs?"

"I don't know, Michael's and Caesar's are pretty nice too."

"Yeah, but theirs don't have white-wall tires like mine. Come on, tell the truth."

I knew what he was up to. Too-Too just wanted me to say exactly what he wanted to hear. He didn't think enough of me to ask if I'd help him build it, so I wasn't going to give it to him.

"I don't think any are da best, they all look good to me." The irony is that I was being truthful.

"You're not being honest." His persistence just made me realize how much it all meant to him.

Summertime was also a time when I could hang out at Mr. Cecil's place. His only child and daughter was a best friend to my sister Pepe. The only times I enjoyed going to the baseball games with Pepe is when Shawana came along. I liked her big afro and she wasn't so wrapped up into baseball like Pepe was. She was good at convincing Pepe to take a break from the game and come out with us to the top of the steep walking ramps. We'd take off running down the ramps yelling, "Chaaaaaarge! Chaaaaaaarge! Chaaaaaaarge!" The gravitational pull on our bodies was exhilarating. I was always the last one to make it down the ramp. I had this fear that I was going to trip and hit the concrete with my face.

Sometimes I spent the night over at Shawana's. Other times, especially when Shawana was out being a teenager, I hung around and kept her eighty-two year old father company. Actually, he probably kept me company more than I kept him. I didn't enjoy spending the night as much as I did visiting. Staying overnight was kind of spooky. Mr. Cecil believed that if he set out a full glass of water every night, Shawana's dead mother would come and drink the water. Apparently, while she was living, Mrs. Cecil would always get up in the middle of the night and drink a glass of water. Unfortunately, Mr. Cecil would leave the glass of water on top of Shawana's dresser. This was the room that I slept in when I stayed over. It was difficult for me to sleep through the night, for my eyes wouldn't shut in fear of the return of her mother.

Squeak.
Bump.
Flush.

Every little noise in the night would start me to meditating. Oh my God, here she comes. That's her—I know it's her, I don't wanna see her. I'd pull the covers over my head. I listened carefully for the sound of footsteps or gulping. I heard neither. Slowly my courage would build. Ok, I'm gonna pull this cover off of my head. The covers slowly came down but I kept my eyelids loosely shut. Then out of curiosity I opened my eyelids just a little bit so I could take a peek. My eyes slowly opened wide. As always, the glass of clear water in the dark room gradually started to turn blue. The light blue water sat motionless. There before me, right in front of my eyes, was a calm ocean. Finally! I pondered, the first sign of daylight. How beautiful to capture the morning sunrise in a glass of water. My eyelids shut tight and I peacefully slept. When I would wake, sometimes half the water would be gone and sometimes none of it would be gone. I always questioned Shawana if the water had not been touched. "Oh, my mama wasn't too thirsty last night." Or she'd say, "She drank some but she only took a sip." Pepe explained to me when there was water missing, Mr. Cecil would sneak into Shawana's room at night and empty out some of the water. However, being naive, I always anticipated the coming of Shawana's dead mother.

I remember very vividly the first time I met old man Mr. Cecil. He was lecturing Shawana and his dentures accidently dropped out of his mouth and onto the floor. I must of jumped out of my shoes. Mr. Cecil got a real kick out of seeing me jump and whenever I visited, before we did anything else, we always went through this kind of ritual sort of thing. For Mr. Cecil, Shawana and Pepe it was all a big thrill, but for me it was something that I felt I could do without.

In I'd step via his front door. Quickly he'd pull out his dentures and start after me. I'd take off and I'd run circles around his kitchen table screaming and yelling my head off. Those teeth seemed to come alive being out of his mouth and I wasn't going to stand around and be the bait. Mr. Cecil plopped those dentures in his mouth and walked away with his belly full of laughter every time.

We mostly watched television or played a game of checkers. Playing checkers with the old man was quite an experience in itself. I always destined the red checkers to be my heroes—just seemed like the perfect color to go along with being female. Mr. Cecil stuck with the black checkers to fight his battles.

With my elbows matted on the tiny wobbly foldaway table, I intensely watched the board. *Jump, double jump.* I sat with my eyebrows cringed wondering how he had done it and why I hadn't seen it coming.

During the beginning and middle of the game, after a victorious move, Mr. Cecil always placed the checkers back into the position that they were in. Then my mentor would repeat his move and reveal his strategy to me. I looked up at him with gratitude and he displayed his pretty white dentures. I never had any problems duplicating his strategies in some of my moves. His shiny, bald head and glaring glasses made him appear mellow and I grew confident that I could take on the geezer. *Jump, double jump, triple jump.* The old man had no qualms about laying it all on me.

A few checkers left on the board. Everytime the game got to this point I got lost. I hadn't the slightest idea as to how I could make my dream come true—wrap up and walk away with a win. I'd stall and stall, hoping that Mr. Cecil would give me a little direction—you know, kinda set me off onto the right path. Intentionally I made my dark brown eyes reach out to him. I was certain that he could hear what they were saying. "But I'm just a little girl, aren't you gonna help me? This isn't fair, you're a big man and I'm just a little girl, you're supposed to let me win." The old geezer just wouldn't bite. I always ended up making a dumb move and geezer's black kings would swallow my red checkers off the board.

I must have played a thousand games of checkers with Mr. Cecil and if I couldn't win on my own, which I never did, he wouldn't let me win at all. I never really got too frustrated for everytime I lost, my mind seemed to expand. I wasn't only playing checkers, moving red chips across a board, I began thinking checkers. I developed new strategies and skills in my head, I learned that little girls had intellect too, that girls were smart enough and could figure things out. I might not have been able to win one over Mr. Cecil but I could beat any other kid in the neighborhood.

Down the tube went my Daddy's theory. Daddy and my seventy-year-old grandmother, Mama's mother, constantly argued and disagreed with one another. She didn't like Daddy too much, thought Mama had made a bad choice. I overheard Daddy many times talking about how stupid, forgetful and senile old people were. Everytime I sat down and played checkers with Mr. Cecil I brought this same speculation with me. I assumed that I would always have the advantage. I learned very fast to respect the geezer's years. Daddy wasn't always right as I had thought.

I always felt comfortable telling Mr. Cecil what was on my mind. Mr. Cecil always had an ear for me and an answer whenever I needed one. I trusted only him with my serious thoughts.

We had just completed an intense game of checkers. It was one of those steamy summer days when the air is so hot one doesn't want to move a limb, not even to go to the bathroom. Thoughts were spinning around in my head and if I didn't get a release I was sure to get a migraine.

"Mr. Cecil, do you believe that there's a God?"

"Sometimes I do, sometimes I don't. Sometimes I will, sometimes I won't." I could tell he had been a smoker before because his voice was low and heavy. It seemed as if he was forcing his words out over a large lump inside his throat. "Depends on da day chile, depends on da day."

"Because sometimes when I drop my candy on da floor I pick it up and say 'I kiss it up to God' then I eat it. I be wondering if da dirt really goes away, you know, if God takes it away."

"Dat be stupid. Only's way you gon git da dirt off is ta wash it. Dat be da thang ta do. If God took da dirt away dat be too easy, den life don't be havin' no meaning. Cuz dats what it be all bout, learnin' ta wash da dirt off yo' self."

"So when I pray, Mr. Cecil, it doesn't matter? Cuz God won't change things anyway?"

"Naw. You gots ta pray, you gots ta pray. Jus gots to be knowin' what ta asks fo' when you prayin'. Why yo' Mama and Daddy be sending ya'll ta school anyhow?"

"So we can learn and be smart."

"Dats right, so you can git somethin' in yo' head. If dey didn't send you ta school and dey sat down, looked up into da sky and said, 'God make my chile smart, make her head full of know-how,' and den dey sat on a stool and waited for it ta happen, jus how smart do you thank you gon be? You'd have so much space up dere in yo head you could fit a bus in it. Dey be waiting fo a train dat ain't gon never show. See, God don't change thangs just like dat." He snapped his finger. "Anyhow some thangs just gon be cuz dey is, dey is what dey is, can't change. If you thank somethin' can be, den ask God to show you how ta do it yo'self. Den praying be matterin.'"

"Do you think I should ask God to show me how to stop my father from hurtin' my mother?"

"Yo Daddy hurtin' you Mama." He took a long pause. "Why?"

"Like when, see a couple of times." I told him a couple of times but there had been more. "I heard my mother tellin' him to stop, that it hurts and I saw him, and Mama was bending over. She kept saying that it hurt. I don't want him to hurt her anymore. Sometimes I wanna talk to her about it and tell her that I want to help her but, somethin' puzzles me."

"What dat be?"

"One time they caught me watching dem and Mama was smiling at me. Even when she says it hurts her there isn't a lot of pain on her face. Everytime they finish Mama comes out of da room smiling. I don't know if she be happy or sad cuz sometimes when I smile I'm really hurtin' inside, like when I go ta school at St. Anne's."

"Did yo'Mama ever cry when you was watching?"

"Nope, never."

Mr. Cecil exhaled and his tensed-up body relaxed in his chair. "How old you be now?"

"Nine."

"Now see, you be too young now ta understand what love be bout. What love be bout between a man and woman is somethin' special, well, dere be a lot thangs dat I cain't explain ta you now. But when you git older and start courtin' boys and when you git married and have a family, you'll understand. You should talk ta yo Mama, tell her hows you feel."

Mr. Cecil was right, there were a lot of things that I didn't understand about love. Mama told me that she wasn't hurtin'.

When I returned to school after summer vacation I sat and listened while my classmates shared their summer ventures.

"My family and I went to Disneyland. I saw Mickey Mouse and Donald Duck. We rode this really neat ride, it was really fun."

There were also trips to Hawaii, Florida and Hollywood. I somehow felt short-changed. However, I thought about Mr. Cecil, my best friend, real hard and then I didn't feel so bad.

Chapter 14

The fall of 1973 was certain to be full of new challenges. I was entering the fourth grade and for some strange reason Daddy was playing a cat and mouse game with the welfare people. They'd send us food stamps and money and Daddy would send it back. They kept sending it and Daddy kept sending it back. We still had food on the table and a place to live so I didn't feel concerned.

"You're gonna have different teachers now, it's not like when you were in the other grades," Sistine explained.

"Yep, you're going to get a different teacher for each subject," Sareeda added.

"I hope you get Miss Tortino for history. She's real nice, I like her. I think she just got married and had a baby," David said.

"Is she old?" I asked.

"No, she's real young and she has long black hair—she's pretty."

We walked past Fabia's store.

I remember so clearly what I felt when I first saw Miss Tortino. Beauty became more than just a word for me, it became well-defined. To me my mother was beautiful but my body had never told me that my mother was beautiful, it was just something that I believed in my mind. Mrs. Tortino's beauty was different for it was a stranger's beauty. Though unpolished, her bright red full lips shined and her long black beautiful hair hung in front of and behind her shoulders. Her thick dark eyebrows were quite alluring. She was a lot younger than the other teachers. She wore black pants and a somewhat loosely fitted blouse—a blouse only a princess would wear. I liked her just by looking at her; my whole body warmed inside. If I had ever seen something or someone so beautiful before, my body had never told me about it. I now looked forward to going to school each day, for I had finally found something worth attending St. Anne's.

"Roof, roof, roof. Roof roof roof roof."

Fabia unhitched the wooden gate. Even after my third year Nicky and Fabia still watched us with curiosity. I couldn't help from staring into Fabia's clear glass refrigerator. How I yearned to add Sayo chocolate milk to my lunch.

Ricky popped some orange slices into his mouth. His pearly whites and bright pink gums stood out from his beautiful dark chocolate skin, like the full moon in a midnight sky. The jelly oozed into the slits between his teeth. Sareeda stormed off into the direction going home. I was amused again.

I peeked around the corner and there he was, the middle-aged robust white man.

"Hi," I said.

He looked up at me. "Hi." As usual he didn't smile, he just looked up at me.

"Bye," I said.

"Bye," he said.

I trampled my way out and caught up with the rest.

When the door cracked open, I picked the dented and bruised apples from the black hand. After the door closed we saw the curtain in the front window move and we all waved.

Phil's crossed eyes bulged behind his trifocals which leaned on the tip of his black nose. Year after year the air in Phil's place seemed to get worse. We put the stale candy in our pockets.

"Pew-ee, it stinks in there," my little brother spoke when we got outside.

No one else said anything. We were out of sight from the red building.

Thunk, thunk!

Pow!

"Ha ha ha."

"Hee hee."

"Nah-nah-nah-nah nah."

Splat!

"Hey Sareeda," I yelled.

Squash.

"Ha ha you missed, I'm mo' git you tomorrow Cindy, just wait."

I stuck my tongue out at Sareeda.

******

I leaned forward to see what it was that was hanging on the side of Nancy Pilchecks' face. She was slowly drifting off to sleep and our teacher, Miss Mary Pat, hadn't noticed yet. I couldn't help but notice the long green yuk that was coming from her nose. I stared at it for a while. As she inhaled, it tried to go back into her nose and as she exhaled it slid further down her face. It looked like a big fat green noodle. I felt rather confused for I had never seen a booger like that before.

Our teacher followed my eyes. "Nancy! Get up and wipe your nose." Nancy, not quite fully alert, brushed her hand across her cheek and smeared the booger on her face. "Nancy! go wipe your nose I said." Yucky yuck, I thought as Nancy passed by my desk. My arms filled with goose pimples.

"Cindy come here," Miss Mary Pat called. She was a rather funny looking lady. She had a head the size of a pea and a body that could cover the earth, if she ever put her arms around it. After the candy incident concerning my little brother, I was a bit wary about being within her line of vision. I stood in front of her as she sat at her desk. My hands were folded together and they rested on my lap. "Yes."

"Don't you ever let me see you do that again!"

"Do what?"

"You know what you did. As long as you're in my class, Miss Cindy, you will never stare at anyone like that again, do you understand?"

"Yes Miss Mary Pat."

"For that type of behavior you will go and stand in the corner and face that blackboard until class is dismissed, do you understand?"

"Yes Miss Mary Pat."

With my head lowered I walked over into the corner. Me and Mr. Cecil played a game of checkers inside that blackboard. My mentor placed the checkers back into the position they were in. He repeated his move and revealed his strategy to me. I looked up at him with gratitude and he displayed his pretty white dentures. "Mr. Cecil, Mr. Cecil, do you want butter on your popcorn?"

Rrrrrrng, rrrrg.

"Class is dismissed." Finally, now I can go to Mrs. Tortino's class.

She glowed in the sunrays that penetrated through our classroom window. Her red lips glistened. So this is what happened to Cinderella, I pondered, she wound up being a history teacher.

She never seems to notice me. Even after I've dug so deep to find the courage to raise my hand, she hardly ever calls on me. I wished that I could be the babysitter for her newborn baby.

******

The cold winter weather of '73 moved in quickly. I joined some other students on a large piece of carpet. I looked around to make sure that everyone else was concentrating on changing their boots. I quickly removed one boot and made sure that I held on to the top of my pearly white sock, which was folded over my toes. I didn't want anyone to see the patches in my sock. Then I made sure again before removing my other boot.

Daddy went out and bought Pepe a used Ford Pinto for her senior year in high school. We sisters and brothers were more than willing to tag along whenever she got ready to go some place. There were Sundays when Mama and Daddy couldn't make it to church and they trusted Pepe to take us in her Pinto. One day, right after Pepe had exited off the busy Walker Expressway, the steering wheel popped right out of its column. There Pepe was trying to make a right turn, holding the steering wheel way up in the air high above the dashboard. Sorry Pepe but cars were not built to work that way. Up until then her extremely compact vehicle took us where we wanted to go.

We siblings piled inside the cream-colored Pinto and headed off to church. We pulled up in front of St. Anne's.

"Somebody had better go in and get the bulletin."

"My clothes don't look right, I'm not going."

"Cindy, go get a bulletin."

"Un un I ain't goin'. All those people are gonna stare at me."

"I went the last time."

"You go!"

"You go!"

"Okay, if nobody goes in, we all are going in and staying!" Pepe said.

After this spoken alternative, someone would eventually run in and take a few service bulletins off of the table in back of the church. Then off to the zoo we went.

My toes froze and thawed, froze and thawed, as we rapidly moved from animal house to animal house. Although they stunk of foul odor, the animal houses were a relief from the zero below temperatures.

"Hey Too-Too, you look just like that hippo."

"Your Mama look just like that hippo," Too-Too responded.

"Yo' Mama is my Mama!"

"No she ain't. Your Mama is that big ugly rhino over there eatin' his mess."

"Un, y'all so nasty."

I liked the lion house the most. I was totally turned off by the manes on the males. All that hair just seemed so out of place to me. It was the female lions that attracted all of my attention. They walked about their cage with grace and I liked the way they stared at me, with those fierce-looking eyes. Their whole existence seemed so beautiful and at the same time so savage. How entrancing.

Before heading back home we rested on the cold benches in the zero below weather. The hot chocolate we got from the concession stands hardly warmed my insides. While I was still sitting, Too-Too stood up in front of me; we were facing one another. Trying to stay warm, he periodically shuffled his feet.

"What would you do if you turned around and Daddy was standing right behind you?" I asked. It was the kind of question that was asked purely out of humor and just a little bit of fear. It was exciting and scary to think that Daddy would creep up on us and catch us in the act. My body tingled all over just thinking about it.

"Pee on myself."

We chuckled at the thought. We both knew that we would all be skinned alive if Daddy appeared. I humorously folded my hands in prayer. "Father forgive us for we have sinned."

"Daddy come around that corner, ain't gon be no time for praying."

"Ha!"

I enjoyed watching our breath form like smoke in the freezing air. I was amazed at how painful the cold air could be, yet at the same time so refreshing. I definitely had preference for it rather than sitting in a pew at St. Anne's.

"Ok what was the gospel about today?" Pepe asked.

"I don't know."

"We have to come up with somethin'."

"Baby Jesus!" I said.

"Ok stupid! Christmas is still a month away." Too-Too said.

"Don't call me stupid."

"Let's say it was about the last supper. The relationship between Judas and Jesus, how Judas betrayed Jesus," Pepe suggested.

"No, no, that has to do with Easter, the gospel wouldn't be about Easter right now— that's way off into next year," Sistine added.

"I think we should stick with baby Jesus. How when Jesus was laying in the crib in the manger and the gifts were presented to him. I don't think it's too early for them to start talkin' about Christmas stuff," Pepe said.

"Jus like I said, baby Jesus!

"Aw shut up."

"Cut it out back there," Pepe demanded. "Ok, that's perfect, baby Jesus it will be."

Before we exited from the car, Pepe made sure that we were all prepared. "Cindy what was the gospel about?"

"Baby Jesus a-way in da maaanger."

"David what was it about?"

"Ba-ba Je-su-su-su-sus."

"Anita."

"Uh the uh, um the manger and da baby uh . . ."

"Ahhhh, you just make sure you don't say nothin', chile," Too-Too teased.

"Sistine!"

"Baby Jesus."

As soon as we walked into the house we handed Daddy the bulletins. "What was the holy gospel about?" he asked. We all got away with another Sunday snow job.

Just like many years before, as soon as the air got cold enough, Daddy attached his hose to a water pipe. He let water flow all over a thick, long, smooth piece of concrete that sat in the middle of the sections of housing rows. We called it the play pen. I watched the older kids, that had ice skates, skate and force the puck across the ice with their homemade hockey sticks.

Smash!

Whoosh.

"Git back, git back, turkey."

"Hey man, woe wooe." *Bam*! Another rump hits the ice.

Broomhead, Freddy and Pepe were always the dominant rivals. They fought over the puck as if it was a token to get into heaven. I wanted a pair of ice skates so badly. One of my friend's parents had bought her a pair of training skates, they had two blades instead of one. I followed that girl around everywhere she went. She never let me use her skates. I, along with some other kids, glided across the ice in our boots and shoes.

******

I opened my eyes and it was Christmas Eve morning, 1973. I couldn't believe it; the day I had waited all year for had finally come. Lucas' shopping cart was a little louder than usual, so I jumped out of bed and took a look out the window. A blizzard was passing through and a shift of wind caught hold of some of the newspapers in Lucas' shopping cart. "Git em Too-Too, git em." Lucas' body was jerking all over the place. Too-Too fought with the wind on the left, then the wind on the right. His dashes seemed helpless against the fierce wind. "Ga-damit ga-damit! Ov-er dere, ov-er dere, git-em Too-Too git-em."

I was in fourth grade and I still wanted to believe in Santa Claus. I had heard much talk that there really wasn't one, plus I had peeked into Mama's and Daddy's closet and seen some toys stashed away. However, I simply couldn't erase from my mind that moment when Broomhead and I had visited Jake's Candy Store a few Christmas Eve's before.

Broomhead lifted me up and sat me on top of a stack of boxes that were next to the candy counter. "See, Santa Claus knows when you be good and when you bad. He lives far away but he can see you and he knows where to bring your toys." My face must have told Broomhead that I wasn't buying it for he quickly leaped to Jake for reassurance. "Right Mr. Jake?" Jake took over. "You see Santa lives far, far a-way." He pointed at the ceiling, then he walked over and turned out the main lights in his store. The silver and gold tinsel that lined the walls and covered the huge Christmas tree glittered brilliantly. The multicolored tree lights bounced a burst of colors onto the deep red candy-filled stockings. Jake looked into my eyes. "He got a crystal ball and he be watchin' to see if you been good or bad, he got a lot little elves helpin him make da toys only fo' the good little girls." My eyebrows raised. It was coming from an adult and I believed it all. My mind became captured. There was no way that I was going to make that moment null and void, regardless of what I had heard about Santa not being real.

I couldn't see it then but now when I look back, I can get a glimpse of Jake's interchanging face. It went from guilty conscience to guilt-free. Clean shaven, light brown skinned Jake saw the fascination in my eyes and couldn't restrain himself from telling all those little white lies. Such a tragic yet wonderful moment—my head full of new knowledge, yet so empty.

Me and my younger brother and sister took our toys up to the bedroom that we three now shared. I neatly sat my dolls upright on the bed. There were small noticeable defects in the dolls like chipped noses and broken arms. They weren't dolls that I had seen on television commercials and wished for. But I didn't want to feel the emotions of concentrating on those things so I made myself overly content. The dolls that sat before me became perfect in every way and I was happy to have them. My sisters and brothers and I had received more gifts this Christmas than ever before. We all agreed that this was going to perhaps be our best Christmas so far.

But, the spirit of Christmas hadn't yet cranked up in our household. Mama and Daddy were anxiously walking the floors because my oldest sister Charlotte and her boyfriend hadn't returned from midnight Mass at St. Anne's. Christmas just wasn't Christmas unless all the siblings were there to share it. I was hoping that my sister would hurry home so that Daddy could put on his Nat King Cole and Burl Ives Christmas records. Their voices always pierced my spirit and gave me a tremendous uplift. Even as I slept during the early morning hours on Christmas day, their voices would remain in my head and I would get a most comfortable sleep.

Shortly after 1:30 a.m. Daddy received a call from the hospital. While we waited around for Daddy to return, the little Christmas spirit that we had took a rapid decline. Good tidings were not expected.

While churchgoers looked on, the smashing of the metal chains left a gash in my sister's upper lip. Her boyfriend received a large number of stitches on the bridge of his nose. They too, like Broomhead, received scars that have become permanent members of their facial features. When was it all going to be over? I couldn't understand how people could be so vile on such a moving day. My dolls didn't look so perfect anymore. There were no melodious voices in my head to carry me off to sleep. I tossed and turned the whole morning.

That following Christmas day Too-Too and I knelt in front of the window and watched the snowflakes pile up. We had the window raised high, and the cold air chilled our faces. A mother held on to her little boy's hand as they struggled through the snow. When they walked in front of our housing unit, Too-Too took what he had said was his best gift ever, a green Gumby doll, and threw it at the little boy. *Wack*! It got him right on the head. We laughed loudly. The mother reached down and picked up the doll from the wet snow. She looked up into our window and wiggled Gumby high in the air. "Nah nah ha ha ah, you ain't gettin' it back. It's mine now, ha ha ha. That's whatcha get!" She handed the doll over to her son. Too-Too cried and cried and cried. "What a stupid, how could you do somethin' so dumb like that for?" I too was brokenhearted.

We all loved that Gumby. I never could understand why he had taken a chance with Gumby. I figure sometimes that maybe all the pain had soaked under his skin. Maybe at that moment when he threw Gumby out the window, nothing really mattered to him anymore. Just maybe I was feeling the same way when I punched that white boy in the ball park.

When I returned to school after Christmas vacation, I had my lies prepared. "So, Cindy would you stand up and please tell us about your Christmas?" my homeroom teacher asked.

"It was really nice. I had a lot of fun."

"What did you get?"

I remembered my favorite television commercial advertisement. "Oh, I got some ice skates, a Barbie doll, a tea set, a Polly doll and a twinkle star doll."

Chapter 15

We arrived at St. Anne's early on the wintery Sunday morning that followed Christmas Day. There were a couple of other early parishioners there, too. The organ keys played on, the harmonious chimes sounded. My ears opened wide to the music. An old lady wearing a black veil lit the multitude of dark red candles that were on both sides of the altar. Inside those orange and blue flames there I was again, within the stained glass windows. I hovered with the saints and walked on top of and through the misty clouds. The saints' presence was as solid as my breath. Silence stood strong and thought was free. I felt so warm inside. It was wonderful.

That next weekend I went to church with Ruby Mae again. It was choir day at M.B. Baptist Church. The men and women in the choir all stood up, revealing their long black robes. A teenage girl stepped from out of the choir and placed herself in front of a microphone. Her voice lifted up, and up and up it went. Her hands floated in front of her as she delivered a sound oh so mellow and sharp. My heart became pierced. Then down came her voice. As it hit the bottom there was a pause in her sound and some charged-up fellow from the audience shouted joyously, "You better sang, Sis-sta!" The choir jumped into an upbeat tempo. The audience and choir clapped their hands in sync. Each time they brought their hands together, the preacher's feet landed on the platform and he let out a loud yelp. *Thump! yeah, thump! yeah, thump! yeah.* My heart pounded along. *Thump! thump! thump!* Then something told me to move. It wasn't a man's voice or woman's voice; perhaps it wasn't a voice at all. It had no origin but it told me to move. "Move! Move! Move!" My hands came together. I was in sync with the rest. There was so much energy that I wanted to be launched. I felt as light as a feather yet strong and sturdy. It was wonderful.

Chapter 16

Although spring, 1974, was around the corner, it felt as though winter was at its peak. So far, fourth grade had been tolerable. I really hoped that when I went on to the fifth grade I would have Mrs. Tortino as one of my teachers.

Moosey and I enjoyed tagging along with Pepe in her Ford Pinto. Most time we didn't have to pester her so much because she was usually generous in taking us around with her. One day she asked us to go over to Paula's house with her. Paula was a classmate of hers from high school. Pepe told us that she had a secret to tell us and that it had something to do with Daddy returning the welfare money. "I'm not going to tell y'all until we're on our way back home."

Paula's parents weren't home so she asked us in. While Paula and Pepe gossiped, Paula's younger brother invited Moosey and me into his bedroom. We sat on his bed and he taught us how to play a card game. He didn't seem to notice or care that our skin color was different than his. I had never felt so welcome into a white person's home before. We played and listened to music for about an hour or so, then Pepe and Paula came running into his bedroom. "Quick! Quick! We have to get out! Their mother and father are coming." It was too late already, we heard the keys being inserted into the front door. "Quick into my bedroom." We ran into Paula's room and hid inside of her tiny closet. We covered our mouths with our hands while we giggled uncontrollably. "Shhh shhh," Pepe said in a whisper. "Every time he comes into the house Paula's father goes straight to the bathroom and he always stays in there for a long time. As soon as he goes in there she's going to sneak us out."

"What about her mother?" I whispered.

"Her mother ain't gonna say anything."

"Ok," Paula said. "Hurry up." We grabbed on to each other's back as if we were a choo-choo train. I was the caboose. We hurried out of the closet laughing. Paula's mother was standing right there. Her eyes opened wide. It looked like they were going to pop out of her head. I thought she was going to fall flat on her face. The thin, grey-eyed Polish mother said in a low and rather confused voice, "Paula, what are those black people doing coming out of your closet?" Our giggling got louder. We hurried towards the front door. When we passed by the bathroom we all held our noses, then out the door we ran.

On the way home Pepe blurted it out. "Daddy is going to buy us a home."

"Un un."

"Yes he is."

"When"

"I don't know but real soon. I already saw the money he has saved up. We're gettin' out of the projects."

"Really?"

"Yeah, I'm not kiddin'. Watch—you'll see."

******

"Ok, let's see, does anyone want to share any of their experiences that they had over the weekend?"

We were taking a pause from our history studies and Mrs. Tortino was allowing us students to take the stage. Peter raised his hand first. "Well, my grandmother made this really neat little sweater for my dog Buffy and when I let him outside to take a walk he ran off. When Buffy came back his sweater was gone and he was all muddy, I think some dogs beat him up and took his sweater." The class chuckled. While my next classmate was telling her story I started to build up a little courage. Go ahead, she's so pretty, this is your chance to speak up so she can notice you, she's so pretty. I know, I can tell her about how I accidentally flushed mom's false teeth down the toilet. I raised my hand. I really didn't want to do it but Mrs. Tortino's beauty was incentive enough. I was aware that I was talking too fast but because of anxiety I couldn't slow down. " . . . and then I must of hit the teeth with my hand and knocked them in the water and flushed the toilet bowl." There was silence. "You flushed the what?!" Mrs. Tortino asked. I swallowed, my voice lowered. "The toilet."

"The what?!" Mrs. Tortino asked again.

I started to feel as though I was using the wrong word. I searched my head for another. "The toilet stool." I blurted out.

"What's that?"

"The seat in the bathroom. I dropped 'em in there and flushed them in the . . ." She interrupted, "Will someone please tell me what she is talking about? I can't understand a word she is saying." Everyone stared at me. I could feel the heat building up in my face. I turned towards Tommy, the kid who always shared his lunches with me. He turned towards me. "You mean in the commode?" he said. I remembered that David had told me that white people didn't say toilet stool. They said commode. "In the commode," I said finally giving Mrs. Tortino what she wanted. She stared at me real hard for a moment. "I don't understand." Then she turned her eyes away from me.

What had I done to make her feel so bad about me? I thought. Beauty being so vile had caught me off guard. I certainly wasn't entranced. How could I have been so stupid and said toilet instead of commode? I asked myself. I was hoping that Pepe was telling the truth about Daddy buying us a home. I didn't want to go on to the fifth grade at St. Anne's, didn't even want to finish the fourth grade there now. Though, I didn't want to ever forget Mrs. Tortino's face—only that humiliating moment.

After school I ran over to Mr. Cecil's. "Mr. Cecil, have you ever seen somethin' so pretty before, you were afraid of it?"

"Why you be afraid of it?" He was too darn clever. Mr. Cecil knew right away that I was having some trouble.

"Well, cuz it's mean to me sometimes and I don't know how to make it happy."

"You talkin' bout somebody you know?"

"Yeah."

"It be da peoples' insides dat matter. Beauty comes from within. Beauty don't be startin' from da outside, gots ta come from da inside ta da outside."

"Then if someone is beautiful on the outside, how can I tell if that beauty has come from da inside or not?"

"Jus watch what dey do and den see how dey act, den you know what dey insides be bout."

"When I go over to dat school in the white people's neighborhood, I be hurtin' all the time and I pray a lot that God will take away that feeling. Should I learn how to take away da pain myself? Is that the secret, Mr. Cecil? Huh? Is that the secret?"

"Dat be da secret."

So then, that is what I'll do, I thought. If we move to a new school I'll take her face and keep it locked in my mind. I'll leave the rest behind.

******

A couple of weeks later, after my embarrassment in Mrs. Tortino's class, all hell broke loose in Teesmith Gardens. Franco Brown's mama came running out of the house screaming, "Ohhh Jesus! God mercy, mercy me. Jesus, oh God, somebody help please, oh Lord dey done almost killed my boy, oh Lord—why why whyyyyy why?" Her cries could have been heard as far as the North Pole. Mrs. Brown was a pretty black woman with light brown eyes and dark brown skin. Though much older she never looked like she was more than thirty. She embraced her stomach as she dropped to her knees on the chilly ground. It was awfully scary and startling to see a mother in so much pain. Mr. Young ran out of his house and tried to help Mrs. Brown up off the ground. "Give me yo' hand, Miss Brown, calm down, now everything gon be alright. Calm down, now everything gon be alright. Calm down now, calm down." In a short time, the whole neighborhood had crowded around to see what was going on. Jesus, there must have been two ambulances and at least twenty-five squad cards in the Garden's parking lot. Sirens were sounding and red and blue lights were flashing all over the place. There were small spots of blood leading up to the Brown's porch and a pool of blood on the front porch. The paramedics worked on Freddy inside the house for quite a while, then they rushed him off to the hospital.

Soon enough everyone in Teesmith had gotten the details on what had happened to Freddy. Two white cops, that were supposedly in custody, had picked up Freddy for curfew. They drove around with him all morning and worked him over pretty good. At nine o'clock that next morning they dumped him on this front porch with a slashed throat. Teesmith was enraged. Some residents gathered up broken pop bottles, baseball bats, knives, iron pipes, etc. They were bloodthirsty for revenge.

"We gon git us some honkeys."

"Dat's right!"

"Da white man done did enough. Dat's right!"

"It's time fo' us ta stand up. Now we gon draw some blood."

"See dat shit dey did ta Freddy. Dey ain't gon do dat no mo', we gone see ta dat, damn pigs."

"Damn pigs!"

"Goddamn pigs!"

The policemen were dressed in their riot gear. A couple of extremely timid black officers tried to talk with and cool down the overheated crowd. I was hurt and angry at the same time. I didn't care, I just wanted to see a white person hurting like Freddy was hurting. It didn't matter—anyone—just as long as they were white. That white boy's eyes didn't look so innocent anymore. I was glad I had kicked that white boy's butt. I simply wanted to get away from all the commotion; it was all too depressing. Mr. Cecil was one of many who had decided to stay put inside of his house. I retreated to his place.

"Did you hear what happened ta Freddy, Mr. Cecil?"

"Yeah I know. Dat's a doggone shame what dey did ta dat boy. Shoot! I'm telling you dis world be somethin' else."

"Did you see all those people out there? Boy, I hope they git somebody. I want somebody white to get killed. I hope they kill a white police."

"Cindy, it hurts my heart ta hear you say dat."

"Why, Mr. Cecil? Dey did it to us, so they should get it back."

"I know, it be stuff happening like dis dat makes you wanna kill somebody. How so easy it be ta feel such a way. Why if men built houses by snapping dey fingers, dey wouldn't be having any muscles to show fo' all da work dey did. As muscles be fo' strength, so be a good thought fo' strength too. If da ideas be of hatred and violence, den da mind be awfully weak. Muscles make fo' a strong body jus as pleasant thoughts make fo' a strong mind. See dis coin?" Mr. Cecil took a silver dollar out of his baggy pants pocket. I nodded. "Now you be havin' three choices. When I throw dis to you you can keep it, throw it back or let it drop on da floor. He tossed me the shiny coin. I caught it. "Ahhh-ha, now see dat coin be in yo' hands now, not mine. What be yo' choice?"

"Uhhh, I'm gonna keep it." I placed the silver dollar in the palm of my hand.

"Dat coin be not in my possession now, it be yours, now you havta decide what ta do wit it. Let's pretend dat dat coin be a pipin' hot stone. I throw it ta you and you catch it. What's gonna happin?"

"I guess I git burned."

"Dat be right. And if you be holdin' it long enough, it be burning a hole right through yo' hand. If I did dat ta you, how you thank you'd feel?"

"I guess I'd be pretty mad at you, Mr. Cecil."

"I bet you would!" he chuckled. "I jus' bet you'd be wantin' ta take dat stone and throw it right back at me, too. Can you believe it, somethin' be so hot dat it can burn through you and many peoples will still hold on ta it? It be jus as easy fo' dem ta hold on ta it as it be fo' you ta wont ta keep dat coin. Den da stone gits hotter and hotter and den dey throw it back cuz dey can't help demselves. Le's take a look outside." We stood behind Mr. Cecil's torn screen door. We could see the parking lot from his unit. "See all dose peoples out dere? Dey all decided to catch da stone dat was thrown ta dem and dey all let it burn a hole right through dey hands. Look at all dose pipes and bottles and bricks. Now dey too be having stones ta throw. See, a hot stone be jus like something evil. A hot stone be like a bunch of flames. When you be seein' dose flames coming, you be havin' a strong mind not ta let them pass through you. If you do, you will git angry and burn a lot of people. And you be burned too, probably worst, cuz you were da creator of dose flames. A lot of dose peoples gon git dey heads busted open and dey ain't gon be havin' nobody ta blame but deyselves.

"But we didn't start da flames—dose police dat beat up Freddy did."

"Yeah, but if you catch da stone, den you be havin' da stone in yo' hands now. You be owner of da flames. Jus like da coin, I threw my coin to you. You caught it. Now it belongs to you. You havta decide if you gon keep it, throw it back or let it drop. If you be lettin' da flames pass through you, den dey will only git bigger. Da best thang ta do be ta let da flames back off away from you. Dey will not be havin' a new body ta grow inside. Dey will have no place ta go, no house ta live in and eventually dey will burn out. If you be acceptin' dem, den you will heat up and throw dem back ta somebody else. Dere be only a few strong minds in dis world and a whole lotta weak ones, so dose flames gon turn into a inferno.

"So what should we do wit' all da anger we feel inside?"

"We havta stand up and fight back but not wit' hot stones. You be already startin' ta fight back by goin' ta school each day. Knowledge be yo' best weapon. Some peoples git know-how so deys can throw hot stones. Please don't do dat. You be sure you git know-how so you can make folks see dat us black peoples be too important ta be havin' our throats cut. If you ever git so mad dat you be feelin' like hurtin' somebody, or if you be wantin' ta jus think about thangs, go somewhere quiet and git yo' thoughts together. Don't be lettin' hatred and bad feelings fo' peoples git da best of you. All dis makes a weak mind and weak mind be makin' a weak body and a weak body be makin' a weak spirit. If all dese dangs be weak, den you be one miserable soul. All dese thangs yo' like ta do—playin' off da wall and goin' to da zoo—you ain't gon be able to even enjoy dose thangs. Yo' troubled mind ain't gon let you. Let yo' mind be free so it can grow. Don't be matterin' if you be white foke green foke or yellow foke. Evil be wantin' everybody ta be a empty head. Be ignant minds da problem, not da color of da skin. I sho' can say, in my days I met a many a white angels, too." Mr. Cecil swayed over to his couch. The old shabby grey bedspread that was covering the holes on the couch moved out of place. He neatly positioned the spread back over the holes and slowly sat down. "You ask?" He pointed towards the ceiling. "Ta show you how ta git rid of da pain?"

"Yeah."

"See. Ask and it'll be given. Look and you be finding, too. See, all dese thangs I jus told you be da start of gittin all da hurt ta go away. Remember, if you be having a coin, you be havin' three choices, but if it be a hot stone, you only have two, ta keep it or let it drop. If you keep da stone den you will automatically throw it back. By da way, I would of kept da coin, too. If somebody throws you a coin, catch it and put it in yo' pocket. Save it fo' a rainy day. If it be a hot stone, let it drop."

Now I understood more about the point Daddy was trying to make to Aunt Ruthie.

A few people that were part of the mob got their heads busted. When they looked around to point their fingers, there was no one to take the blame. And so the judge said, "The officers were just protecting themselves from a bunch of . . ."—angry people with hot stones to throw. I imagined that some of the cops were weak and some were strong, that some police officers went home and gave their families and friends hell, because of the stressful day they had, while other officers simply dropped their stones.

Freddy lived, but I will never hear him speak; I will never hear him sing Elvis Presley tunes again. His vocal cord had ben slit. "Anybody want da rest of dese french fries?" I will always hear it over and over and over again. And I will always answer, oooh give em ta me, Freddy.

Chapter 17

It all happened so fast. Pepe returned home from riding around with Mama and Daddy all day. She jumped up and down with excitement. "Y'all oooh it is so bad. It's got a basement and a gigantic back yard. It sits on a hill where all the rich people live in Sancho Hills, it is so bad. Oh God! I can't believe it." My idea of what a house looked like in Sancho Hills came from a cartoon that I watched on television called "The Flintstones." I imagined that our new house was built of Stone Age rocks and our neighbors sat on their front porches in rocking chairs, holding shotguns in their hands.

"Are there any hillbillies there?" I asked. Hillbillies was a word I used to describe the characters that I had seen sitting on their front porches, holding guns and shooting the chitchat.

"Yep, there's hillbillies there too," Pepe said. I lit up with excitement. I felt that a place like Bedrock, according to the cartoon, would be a pretty cool place to live.

Daddy took me along with him to the bank. We sat at a big desk in the middle of the bank floor. The white lady slid a small stack of forms in front of Daddy. He started to look over them. "Here, what do this say?" he pointed to the paragraphs. I read halfway through the clauses, until Daddy felt the rhythm of the information that I was reading to him. "Ok," he spoke in a low voice while nodding his head forward. "Where do I write my name?" I looked for the word signature and the small black x. I pointed to the line.

"Here?"

"Yes, Daddy."

"And the date go here?"

"Yes."

The office lady stared at us over her glasses that hung halfway down her face. I tried to avoid looking up at her. I was ashamed that my Daddy couldn't read.

Daddy signed all the final papers. We all piled into our station wagon and Daddy drove us up to Sancho Hills to see our new home. Sancho was forty miles southwest from Teesmith Gardens. There were no Stone Age rock-built houses. I also didn't see any hillbillies neither. Our home sat on a piece of land that was just a tiny bit elevated but it wasn't on a big hill. Daddy drove us through the neighborhood and there were some homes a little further west from us that sat on the top of steep hills; this was where all the rich people lived. Compared to those homes our house was definitely on flat landscape. I was disappointed, not with our house but realizing that Pepe had played with my imagination. Even so, my excitement about moving into our new home overshadowed my disappointment.

The day came for us to pack our things and move on to our new residence. I ran over to say my good-bye to Mr. Cecil. In I stepped via the front door. Mr. Cecil was sitting on his couch watching television. He turned and glanced at me, then turned back to the television. I meditated. Come on, aren't you gonna come after me just this one last time? Mr. Cecil just stared at his television set. I figured that there wasn't going to be any running around that kitchen table, screaming and yelling my head off, for just this one last time. I went and sat next to Mr. Cecil. There was a silly game show on television, a game show that he had told me he hated sometime before. I didn't think that he believed in God at this moment. His place wasn't as neat as usual. He had left some things lying about. The holes in the couch were exposed. The dull green-painted walls seemed a lot dimmer, too. The lamp, the foldaway table, the snowy-pictured television with no antenna, and everything there all seemed so alone now. Then again maybe it was just me. Maybe everything was like it had always been. Just maybe I hadn't really noticed it all until then. "Jus' come to say good-bye, Mr. Cecil. Thanks for teaching me how to play checkers. I'll be seeing you. I have to go now, my Daddy is fixin' to leave." Using the arm of the couch for leverage, Mr. Cecil stood up on his frail legs. He swayed back to the couch. He gave me the checker board that we always played on, and he handed me the checkers in a brown paper bag that had my name on it. I was wrong before, I thought. He did believe. I think he believes all the time. "Thanks Mr. Cecil, thank you very much Mr. Cecil!" I was so excited about getting out of the projects, I just wanted to fly away. I started towards the front door.

"Tell you mama and daddy I say God bless."

"Ok, good-bye."

Had I known back then the true value of what I was leaving behind, I would have hugged Mr. Cecil tightly, told him that I loved him and would have given him a big kiss right on the top of his shiny, bald head.

"Here now, take this out there and say good-bye ta all your friends." Daddy handed me a large box of candy.

"Ok."

"Y'all house be real big?" Ruby Mae asked.

"Yep, it's got a basement and a big back yard too."

"A yard! A basement? Boy ya'll be so lucky, y'all got a lotta money y'all so rich!" Ruby Mae said enviously.

Through her voice I felt like I was being let out of a cage. I looked back inside that cage for a moment. I saw Ruby Mae.

"No, we not rich. My Daddy was in a train wreck a long time ago and he got some money from that. That's how come we got a house. Plus a lotta nice people helped my Daddy get the house." I was telling her the truth. "Here." I gave Ruby Mae the box with a few pieces of candy left inside. "You can have the whole thing. I don't want anymore. I'm getting a stomach ache."

"Da whole thang? Even da box?"

"Uh huh."

Daddy managed to get his station wagon parked illegally on the large piece of concrete, the play pen. Me, Too-Too, and Broomhead helped Daddy load up the remainder of our belongings. The stuff weighed down our car so Daddy had to drive real slow. When we pulled out onto the street a few of our friends ran alongside our car.

"Bye Too-Too," Franco yelled.

"See y'all later." Ruby Mae waved.

"Take it easy Broomhead."

"See y'all." Broomhead waved.

"Bye-bye."

Daddy sped up and our friends couldn't keep up anymore. I looked at their faces real hard so that I wouldn't forget. They soon became specs on the side of the traveling road.

Chapter 18

On one end of our new block lived mostly blacks and on the other end it was mostly whites. Our house was almost in the middle of the block. The white people were selling their homes real fast.

Daddy told us that we were going to have to take the el train to St. Anne's until he could get us into a Catholic school out by our new home. Summer came and went and the new school year started up. When it got cold and the snow started to stick, life became really miserable. We had to get up two hours earlier than usual and trudge through the thick snow. We walked six blocks before we got to our first bus. Then we took the crowded el train and two more buses.

There was no passing by Phil's store or the warehouse or Fabia's store. The bus route took us through a totally different section. I missed the walks we had; I missed walking underneath that viaduct and the sounds of those landing apples. I even missed the stinky smell in Phil's store.

We were always late. It was awful having to stand in Sister Mary's office and wait for her to write us out tardy slips. She looked at us as if we were criminals. A couple of times she called the head priest even though we were standing right in front of her. "But I don't think that this is fair. If we continue to allow them to do this then all the other students are going to want the same." He must have told her to shut her chops because she always ended up giving us tardy slips anyway.

We stayed out of St. Anne's for one day so that Daddy could take us around to different schools. Our first stop was at St. Anitas, which was a few blocks west of us, on the bottom of the steep hills in Sancho. On our way in, there were a group of white boys exiting. They all looked like they were on the football team. There was an uproar after they saw us. The nun that came to greet us tried to settle them down. "Come on boys, keep it down. You know that isn't polite, keep it down." When we passed by the classrooms the lessons stopped and the curious white faces peeked out the open doors at us. There wasn't another black face in sight. The nun led us to an office.

"Well, Mr. Roberts, I have spoken with Sister Mary from St. Anne's and I did inform her that we only have a limited amount of space available." Daddy looked straight into the nun's eyes. "Uh, we only have an opening for your youngest, the one in second grade, uh, all the other classes are filled."

"Well, I would really hate to have to send her here by herself. You know, the kids are use to going to school together."

"The only other alternative I can suggest to you, Mr. Roberts, is that you go over to St. Ellas. It's possible that they may have some openings. I believe it's a little closer to your home." She handed Daddy the address. "I'll give them a call and let them know that you are on your way."

Daddy didn't take us in with him this time. We all sat in the car and waited. St. Ellas was on the east side of our home. Most of the whites who had lived on the east side had already flighted out to the west side of Sancho. St. Ellas was quickly becoming populated by Blacks.

Daddy came back to the car looking pretty sad. "Well kids, looks like I'm gonna havta send ya'll ta public school. They're filled up, too. Ya'll wanna go ta public school?" Only thing we really knew about public schools was that we didn't have to wear uniforms. Because most of our black friends in our new neighborhood, like our friends in the projects, went to public school, we told Daddy that we preferred going to a non-private school. Didn't look like we had much of a choice anyway.

Arrangements were made for us to transfer out of St. Anne's and into Sanders Public School. Sanders was only a couple of blocks up the street from our home. On my last day at St. Anne's I felt more than eager to be leaving this school behind. We headed for home before the school day had ended. On my way out of my classroom Mrs. Raydon, my fifth grade teacher who had also been my first grade teacher, told the students to say goodbye. She explained to them that I wasn't coming back. I stood in the middle of the floor with all my belongings in my hand. Some of the students waved and said good-bye. I waved back. I turned and walked towards the door. "Cindy," Mrs. Raydon called. I turned back. "Would you please write us? We'd really like to hear how everything is going for you." "Yeah," one of the students added. I hesitated for a moment. "Ok" I said.

I couldn't believe it, they were actually asking me to write. No way! I don't wanna have anything to do with this place anymore. Besides, at that moment, I felt that Mrs. Raydon was just being polite; that they didn't really care one way or the other how things would turn out for me.

The bus pulled out from the street corner. I stared out the window looking back. My mind reminisced. The chimes and the organs will play on. Fabia's dog will bark and Mrs. Tortino will break to let her students take the stage. There will be talent show nights and baseball games. Black boys will wipe away at dirty windows trying to find something inside themselves to appreciate. I could see the piano in the corner, the chairs and all the rest of those instruments; my nostrils filled with the strong smell of wood. The bus passed by the closed Lions baseball park. I could hear the screams from the crowd inside. Someone else is sleeping in the bedroom that I use to sleep in. Imagine that! I thought.

Chapter 19

Sanders was seventy-five percent black and twenty-five percent white. Sanders had a fire drill just like the one at St. Anne's. Although so faraway, those dongs from Dalbot still haunted me. No matter how much I tried I couldn't get those dongs to leave my mind. I seemed attached to them. I constantly questioned myself. Why did St. Anne's and Sanders have bzzzz fire drills while Dalbot had those loud shrilling dongs? Had those dongs been planted for my destiny?

Although we didn't go to school at St. Anitas, on the west side of Sancho, we attended church there. They definitely weren't accustomed to black folks on the St. Anitas side of town. Whenever we got the chance, we snuck off on our Sunday visits to the zoo.

I never wrote my classmates at St. Anne's. In the letter that I should have sent, I'd thank Mrs. Raydon for having patience with me. I'd let her know how important it was for me, for her to look beyond and encourage me to learn. I would thank Tommy for sharing his lunches with me and always showing compassion toward me. I'd tell Mrs. Tortino that I had made a mistake, that I hadn't accidently flushed my mama's teeth down the toilet bowl, that my mama had found them on a shelf, which was right next to the toilet bowl. To those that this applied to, I would tell them that I did have it and I will always have it. And that they should have touched me and caught it cuz they didn't know what they were missin'. Certainly I'd end my letter by sincerely wishing them all a blessed and prosperous life.

I wish I had a magic wand so I could go back and dig out those Lion emblem cushions from the trash. I wish I could find that boy and give him back his seat cushions.

I didn't see Mr. Cecil again until a year after we had moved away. Had on a dark grey suit with a matching tie. The old man was looking pretty sharp, his daughter had him fixed up and real nice. However, I didn't like his wooden casket. I thought he deserved a gold one.

I drifted back to that day when I had said good-bye to him. I felt so empty inside because I hadn't hugged him. You know, I have this deep inner feeling, that someday me and Mr. Cecil are gonna meet again. We're gonna sit down and play a game of checkers, a real heavy game of checkers.. Until then I'm gonna practice real hard. And you know what? I'm gonna beat that geezer.

Epilogue

"Come on girl and show me howta do the funky chicken."

"Aunt Ruthie, I'm fifteen years old, I don't do the funky chicken anymore. That one been tired out a long time ago." I finished rinsing and drying my last dishes.

"Look at ya! Ain't got a ounce a soul left in ya. I told dat fool. Cindy, you knock-kneed and you walk like the dead. Why hell! A penguin got more umph than you do."

"Aunt Ruthie, you haven't started back to drinking again this morning, have you?"

"Yep."

"Aunt Ruthie."

"I had two colas and a glass of milk." She picked at her teeth with a toothpick.

"Honest?"

"Honest girl."

"Okay, put on some James Brown—I'll do the funky chicken alright. I can do the funky chicken so good...."

Aunt Ruthie waltzed over to the stereo with the toothpick hanging from her mouth. She plopped down an LP, and tapping her feet to the music she stepped back to watch me.

"Aunt Ruthie! I thought you were gonna put on some James Brown. I cain't do no funky chicken to, 'Hey Jude'!" I grabbed my jacket from the couch. "Really Ruthie, I hafta go. My friends are waiting for me down in the car. I'll show you another time." I ducked underneath Ruthie's soft punch as I continued out the door.

"Yeah right. The world woulda' done been ended by the time you cain't do the funky chicken to 'Hey Jude.' Why hell, where I comes from peoples can do the funky chicken to whale music. The chile is pitiful. Lord, what dis here world be comin' to? I jus' don't know." She continued to talk to herself. "I'd rather she be a penguin."